To Donna, a winter's child, with love
~ K. W.

For my cousin Grace
~ A. E.

Copyright © 2011 by Good Books, Intercourse, PA 17534
International Standard Book Number: 978-1-56148-729-5

Text copyright © Kathryn White 2011
Illustrations copyright © Alison Edgson 2011
Original edition published in English by Little Tiger Press,
an imprint of Magi Publications, London, England, 2011
LTP/1500/0221/0411 • Printed in Singapore

Cataloging-in-Publication data available from the Good Books website.

When Will It Snow?

Kathryn White • Alison Edgson

Intercourse, PA 17534, 800/762-7171, www.GoodBooks.com

"Winter is coming, Little Bear," Mother Bear
said. "Soon icy winds will blow, bringing soft,
white snow. We must snuggle down to sleep,
safe in our den."

"I don't want to sleep," said Little Bear.
"I want to play in the snow!"

Then he bounded away to hide.

"Oooh, I love hide-and-seek!" cried
Squirrel, peeping down from a tree.
"Sshhh!" Little Bear hushed.
"I'm not playing hide-and-seek.
I've run away."

Mole popped up with a "Boo!"

Little Bear stamped his foot, "I'm not playing, I'm hiding. If I go home, I'll have to sleep for the whole winter. And I'll *never* know what snow is like."

"I'll show you what snow's like," chuckled Squirrel. "It falls from the sky, like this." And she tossed acorns into the air.

"Snow doesn't bounce like that!"
cried Mole. "Snow is soft and
wet—like this!"

He wiggled his bottom and
dived into a puddle. *Sploosh!*
Little Bear squealed with delight.

"Snow is thick," said Squirrel. "You
can make snowmen with it and . . .
SNOWBALLS!" And she tossed
a ball of mud towards her friend.

Little Bear ducked but . . .

the mud-ball splatted over
poor Mole!

Suddenly mud-balls
flew everywhere.

"You can make angel wings in snow," said Squirrel, falling backwards and flapping her arms.

"I can do that, too," whooped Little Bear as he and Mole joined in.

Soon angel wings covered the ground.

Bear looked at his friends. "Will you two play in the snow while I'm asleep?" he asked.

"Oh, yeah!" said Mole. "Hide-and-seek is great in the snow."

Just then Little Bear heard his mother calling.
He flopped down in a huff.

"Grouchy grizzly!" giggled Mole, making
him a funny hat.

"Don't forget me," said Bear.

"'Course not!" said Squirrel.

But Bear's friends were already playing without him.

Mother Bear reached out for
a hug.

"I don't want hugs,"
said Bear. "I want to play in
the snow."

"We bears sleep through the winter,"
said Mother Bear softly. "And when
we wake, the cold snow is gone."

"Will my friends be gone, too?"
whispered Little Bear.

"True friends are always there for
you, like the sunshine," said Mother
Bear snuggling Little Bear into bed.

Outside the cave, soft snow fell
all through the long winter.

Then one day, when the spring sunshine had melted the last of the snowflakes, Mother Bear gently shook Little Bear awake.

"Spring is here, Little One," she said.

Bear raced outside. The world was warm and filled with the scent of blossoms and fresh grass.

Bear ran straight to the muddy puddle to look for Squirrel and Mole.

"They've gone," he sighed. "They've forgotten all about me."

Just then, Little Bear heard
a laugh. He quietly tiptoed
through the trees . . .

Bridges Grade 4
Home Connections

Unit 1
Multiplicative Thinking

Unit 2
Multi-Digit Multiplication & Early Division

Unit 3
Fractions & Decimals

Unit 4
Addition, Subtraction & Measurement

Unit 5
Geometry & Measurement

Unit 6
Multiplication & Division, Data & Fractions

Unit 7
Reviewing & Extending Fractions, Decimals & Multi-Digit Multiplication

Unit 8
Playground Design

NAME David Carmona Jr | DATE

 Number Line Puzzles page 1 of 2

Note to Families

Students can use number lines to review the multiplication facts they learned in third grade. Number lines can help students use facts they know to help them figure facts they don't remember. Talk together about relationships between facts that you see in the two number lines below, such as numbers that double.

1 Fill in the blanks in the number lines.

a

| 2×4 | 3×4 | 4×4 | | 8×4 | 9×4 | 10×4 |
| 8 | 12 | 16 | | 32 | 36 | 40 |

b

| 2×8 | 3×8 | 4×8 | | 8×8 | 9×8 | 10×8 |
| 16 | 24 | 32 | | 64 | 72 | 80 |

2 Complete the facts.

8	8	8	8	8	7	7
×2	×4	×8	×10	×9	×10	×9
16	32	64	80	72	70	63

3 Roger's little brother, Saul, wants to know if $5 \times 7 = 7 \times 5$. If you were Roger, how would you explain to Saul whether the equation is true?

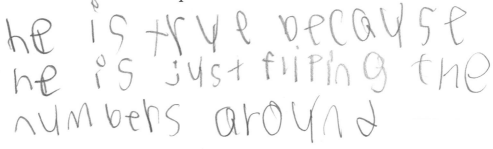

he is true because he is just fliping the numbers around

(continued on next page)

4 Each of the 29 students in Mr. Brown's fourth grade brought 2 notebooks to class the first day of school. How many notebooks was that in all? Show your thinking with numbers, sketches, or words. Then write an equation that represents your work.

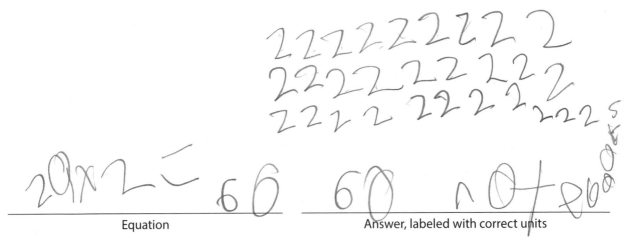

2 2 2 2 2 2 2 2 2
2 2 2 2 2 2 2 2 2 2
2 2 2 2 2 2 2 2 2 2 2 5

29 x 2 = 60   60 notebooks

_____   _____
Equation   Answer, labeled with correct units

5 Each of the students in Mr. Smith's class also brought in 3 pocket folders. Mr. Smith wrote a multiplication equation to compare the number of students to the number of pocket folders they brought in. Fill in the bubble to show what this equation means.

$$87 = 3 \times 29$$

○ 87 is 3 more than 29

◉ 87 is 3 times as many as 29

○ 29 is 3 times as many as 87

6 **CHALLENGE** If 5 students each brought in 8 boxes with 10 pencils per box, and 10 students each brought in 8 boxes with 5 pencils per box, how many total pencils did the students bring in? Show your thinking with numbers, sketches, or words.

_____   _____
Equation   Answer, labeled with correct units

NAME _____ | DATE _____

 Models for Multiplication page 1 of 2

Write a story situation to go with each multiplication model.

Multiplication Model	Story
ex $2 \times 3 = 6$	Keith's dog, Spot, ate 2 cans of dog food every day for 3 days in a row. Spot ate 6 cans of dog food in 3 days.
1 $7 \times 6 = 42$	
2 $4 \times 4 = 16$	
3 $4 \times 6 = 24$	
4	

Number of _____	1	2	4	8
Number of _____	6	12	24	06

(continued on next page)

NAME _____ | **DATE** _____

Models for Multiplication page 2 of 2

	Multiplication Model	Story
5	$5 \times 6 = 30$	
6	$8 \times 9 = 72$	

7   There are 4 rows of crayons in this box. Each row has the same number of crayons. How many crayons are in the box? Show your thinking.

8   Teachers collected $5 from each of the 130 fourth grade students at the beginning of the year for field trips. The first field trip cost $120. The second field trip cost $250. How much can they spend on the last field trip if they need to have $25 left over to wash the bus? Show your thinking using words, numbers, or pictures.

NAME _____ | DATE _____

 Modeling Multiplication & Division page 1 of 2

For problems 1 and 2, complete the sketches and write the equations.

1

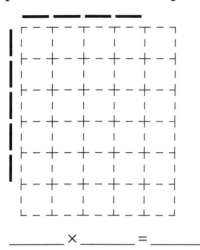

_____ × _____ = _____

2

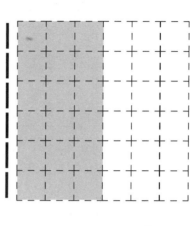

_____ ÷ _____ = 3

3 Copy one equation from above and write a story problem to go with it.

ex I bought 5 packs of pencils. Each pack had 4 pencils in it. How many pencils did I get? (5 × 4 = 20)

Complete the number line and ratio table.

4

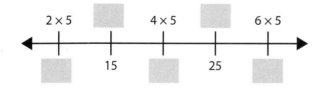

5

1	2		4	5		7	
3	6	9		15	18	21	24

(continued on next page)

Modeling Multiplication & Division page 2 of 2

6 Mr. Still's class has music for 50 minutes and then independent reading for 20 minutes. Music starts at 8:30. What time does Mr. Still's class finish independent reading?

7 Ms. Ford's class starts art at 9:30 and finishes at 10:15. They spend twice as much time in math class. If they start math at 1:10, what time do they finish math?

Factors & Tea Lights page 1 of 2

1 Imagine using 48 tiles to build each rectangle below. Write in the missing dimensions on the rectangle sketches.

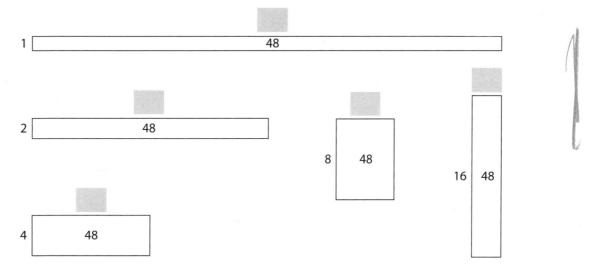

2 The factors of 48 are:

1 and _____   2 and _____   4 and _____   8 and _____   16 and _____

3 a Is 48 a prime number or a composite number?

b How do you know?

4 Study your list of factors for 48. What patterns do you observe?

(continued on next page)

Factors & Tea Lights page 2 of 2

5 Write the missing parts on this number line:

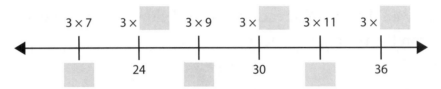

6 Tea light candles are being packaged 6 to a box. Fill in the table:

Number of Boxes	4		6	7		9	
Total Number of Candles	24	30			48		60

For the problems below, use numbers, words, or labeled sketches to explain your answers.

7 Jane has 7 tea light candles. Aisha has 5 times more candles than Jane. How many candles does Aisha have?

8 Theo has 50 tea light candles. Madeline has half as many candles as Theo. How many candles does Madeline have?

NAME _____ | DATE _____

 Multiplication Fact Strategies page 1 of 2

Doubles Plus One Set Facts

When one of the factors is 3, you can think about the Doubles fact, and then add one more set of the number being doubled. For example, 6×3 is 6 doubled (12) plus one more set of 6.

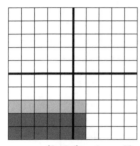

$3 \times 6 =$ ___ $(2 \times 6) + 6$ $12 + 6 = \textbf{18}$

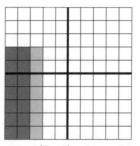

$7 \times 3 =$ ___ $(7 \times 2) = 14$ $14 + 7 = \textbf{21}$

You can use this strategy with larger numbers, too:

$3 \times 25 =$ ___ $(2 \times 25) + 25$ $50 + 25 = \textbf{75}$

$150 \times 3 =$ ___ $(2 \times 150) + 150$ $300 + 150 = \textbf{450}$

1 Shade in the areas and complete the equations.

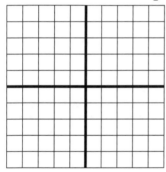

$3 \times 5 =$ _____

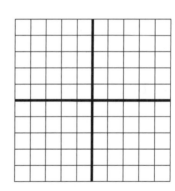

$3 \times 8 =$ _____

2 If you had 2 boxes of 8 crayons and your teacher gave you another box of 8 crayons, how many crayons would you have?

3 Cody bought 2 bags of 5 apples. He already had 1 bag of 5 apples at home. How many apples does Cody have in all?

4 Write a story problem for a Doubles Plus One Set (×3) fact.

(continued on next page)

NAME _____ | DATE _____

Multiplication Fact Strategies page 2 of 2

Tens Facts

5 Circle the groups of 10 in the arrays below, and solve the equations.

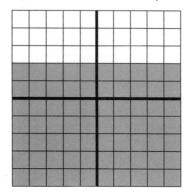 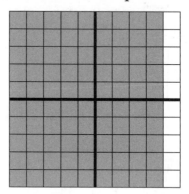

$7 \times 10 =$ _____ $10 \times 9 =$ _____

When you understand place value, multiplying larger numbers by 10 can be easy, too.

$10 \times 25 = 250$ $670 \times 10 = 6700$

Half-Tens Facts

When one of the factors is 5, you can multiply the other factor by 10 and then divide the answer in half.

6 Fill in the blanks below.

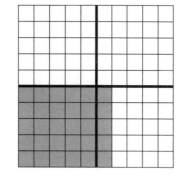

$5 \times 6 =$ _____ $6 \times 10 = 60$ Half of 60 is _____

Half-Tens Facts

n	$\times 10$	$\times 5$
1	10	5
2		
	30	
4	40	
5		25
6		

7 Max had 6 dimes in his pocket. How much money did he have?

8 Jose had 7 nickels in his pocket. How much money did he have?

9 If Suzie bought 9 baskets with 5 large peaches in each basket, how many peaches did she buy?

NAME _____ | DATE _____

 Multiplying by 8 & 9 page 1 of 2

1 Circle all the Double-Double-Doubles facts (×8) in blue. Then solve them and use a regular pencil to write each product.

2 Circle all the Tens Minus One Set facts (×9) in red. Then solve them and use a regular pencil to write each product.

6	9	7	7	5
× 9	× 4	× 8	× 9	× 8

3	4	9	8	9
× 9	× 8	× 6	× 8	× 9

3 a Pick one fact from above and write it here: _____.

b Color in the array for that fact on the grid below.

c Label the array to show how you found the product, and use equations or words to explain your work.

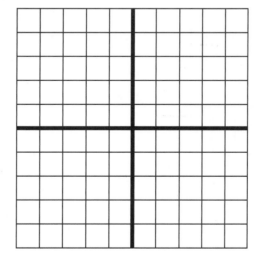

(continued on next page)

11

Multiplying by 8 & 9 page 2 of 2

4 Shade in and label the arrays of two more Double-Double-Double facts in the grids below. Write an equation for each fact.

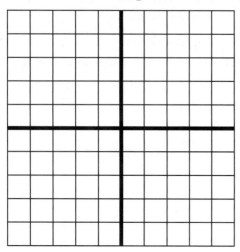 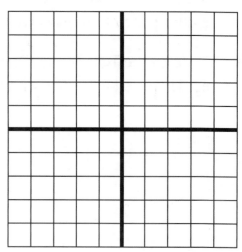

5 Shade in and label the arrays of two more Tens Minus One Set facts in the grids below. Write an equation for each fact.

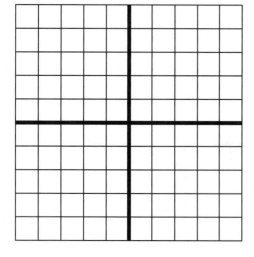 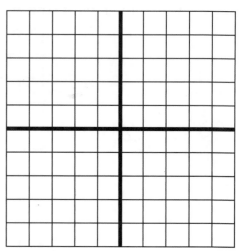

NAME Darid Carmona Jr (hw) | DATE

 Multiples, Flowers & Cards page 1 of 2

1 When you count by a number, you are naming the multiples of that number. For example, if you skip-count by 5s, you are naming the multiples of 5: 5, 10, 15, 20, 25, and so on. In each sequence below, fill in the missing multiples.

ex 5, 10, 15, __20__, 25, 30, __35__   **a** 3, 6, __9__, 12, 15, 18, __21__, 24

b 6, __12__, 18, __24__, 30   **c** 9, 18, __27__, 36, 45, __54__, 63

2 Circle all the multiples of the number in each box.

ex	5	16	(20)	(15)	42	36	(45)	18
b	4	8	6	14	16	20	28	19
d	8	28	32	48	16	60	72	19

a	2	(5)	6	7	8	14	21	(10)
c	7	22	33	(21)	14	16	42	35
e	3	(21)	35	18	36	44	12	29

3 Fill in the missing numbers.

$$\begin{array}{r} 9 \\ \times\,9 \\ \hline \blacksquare \end{array} \qquad \begin{array}{r} 3 \\ \times\,9 \\ \hline \blacksquare \end{array} \qquad \begin{array}{r} 4 \\ \times\,4 \\ \hline \blacksquare \end{array} \qquad \begin{array}{r} 2 \\ \times\,6 \\ \hline \blacksquare \end{array} \qquad \begin{array}{r} 7 \\ \times\,8 \\ \hline \blacksquare \end{array}$$

$$\begin{array}{r} 3 \\ \times\,\blacksquare \\ \hline 24 \end{array} \qquad \begin{array}{r} 7 \\ \times\,\blacksquare \\ \hline 14 \end{array} \qquad \begin{array}{r} \blacksquare \\ \times\,5 \\ \hline 30 \end{array} \qquad \begin{array}{r} \blacksquare \\ \times\,4 \\ \hline 36 \end{array} \qquad \begin{array}{r} 3 \\ \times\,\blacksquare \\ \hline 12 \end{array}$$

$$\begin{array}{r} 6 \\ \times\,2 \\ \hline \blacksquare \end{array} \qquad \begin{array}{r} 6 \\ \times\,4 \\ \hline \blacksquare \end{array} \qquad \begin{array}{r} 6 \\ \times\,8 \\ \hline \blacksquare \end{array} \qquad \begin{array}{r} 6 \\ \times\,16 \\ \hline \blacksquare \end{array} \qquad \begin{array}{r} 6 \\ \times\,32 \\ \hline \blacksquare \end{array}$$

(continued on next page)

Multiples, Flowers & Cards page 2 of 2

4 Four friends were making cards to sell at the holiday sale. Each friend made 9 cards. They put all their cards together and then bundled them in groups of 6 cards to sell. How many bundles of 6 cards did they make? Show all your work.

5 **CHALLENGE** Zack measured a rectangular garden at the park. The longer sides each measured 15 feet and were 3 times longer than the shorter sides. If Zack walked all the way around the garden, how far did he walk?

🏠 Arrays & Factors page 1 of 2

1 Draw and label a rectangular array to show two factors for each number. Do not use 1 as a factor. Then write the fact family that goes with each array that you draw.

ex 8

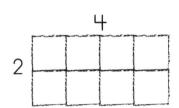

$\underline{\ 2\ } \times \underline{\ 4\ } = \underline{\ 8\ }$

$\underline{\ 4\ } \times \underline{\ 2\ } = \underline{\ 8\ }$

$\underline{\ 8\ } \div \underline{\ 4\ } = \underline{\ 2\ }$

$\underline{\ 8\ } \div \underline{\ 2\ } = \underline{\ 4\ }$

a 16

_____ × _____ = _____

_____ × _____ = _____

_____ ÷ _____ = _____

_____ ÷ _____ = _____

b 18

_____ × _____ = _____

_____ × _____ = _____

_____ ÷ _____ = _____

_____ ÷ _____ = _____

2 List all the factors of each number below.

ex 12	1, 2, 3, 4, 6, 12	**a** 16	
b 17		**c** 24	
d 9		**e** 36	

3 Circle the prime number(s) in problem 2.

    a Draw a square around the square number(s) in problem 2.

(continued on next page)

Arrays & Factors page 2 of 2

4 Is the number 25 prime or composite? How do you know?

5 Judy has a collection of 30 stamps. She can divide the stamps into 2 equal groups of 15 stamps. What are two other ways she could divide the stamps into equal groups?

6 **CHALLENGE** Judy's brother Sam has a collection of 96 comic books. What are the ten ways Sam could divide his comic books into equal groups?

Measuring Lengths page 1 of 2

1 Would you use centimeters or meters to measure the length of

a your bedroom? _____

b your big toe? _____

c a car? _____

d a mouse? _____

e the gym? _____

2 Fill in the table below to convert between centimeters and meters. The first 2 rows are done for you.

centimeters (cm)	meters (m)
100 cm	1 m
200 cm	2 m
300 cm	
	8 m
2500 cm	
	31 m

3 For each of the following story problems, show your work using numbers, labeled sketches, or words. Write an equation, including the answer labeled with the correct units, to represent your work.

a Chloe is a baby who is 24 inches tall. Her father is 3 times as tall as she is. How many inches tall is Chloe's father?

(continued on next page)

Measuring Lengths page 2 of 2

b Chloe's dog, Wilson, is 27 inches long. Chloe's hammock is 4 times as long as Wilson. How many inches long is the hammock?

4 CHALLENGE A small table is 2 feet by 3 feet. A large table is twice as long and twice as wide as the small table. What is the area of the large table in square feet?

NAME _____ | DATE _____

 Mass & Volume Story Problems page 1 of 2

For each problem, show your thinking with numbers, sketches, or words. Then write an equation that represents your work.

1 DJ and Tyler are watering plants. DJ uses 18 liters of water. Tyler uses 5 times as much water. How much water does Tyler use?

_____   _____
            Equation   Answer, labeled with correct units

2 Chris and Jocelyn are building a patio out of bricks. Chris uses 23 kilograms of bricks. Jocelyn uses 6 times as many kilograms. How many kilograms of bricks does Jocelyn use?

_____   _____
            Equation   Answer, labeled with correct units

3 The mass of one bouncy ball is 14 grams. Tracy has 8 bouncy balls. What is the mass of all 8 bouncy balls?

_____   _____
            Equation   Answer, labeled with correct units

4 True or False?

a A liter is 1,000 times as much as a milliliter. _____

b A gram is 300 times smaller than a kilogram. _____

c There are 99 centimeters in a meter. _____

5 Fill in the bubble to show which unit you would use to measure the amount of water in a very large pitcher.

   ◯ milliliter   ◯ kilogram   ◯ liter   ◯ centimeter

(continued on next page)

Mass & Volume Story Problems page 2 of 2

6 Fill in the bubble to show which unit you would use to measure the mass of a mouse.
○ centimeter   ○ gram   ○ liter   ○ kilogram

7 **CHALLENGE** Anna has 15 stickers. Rosa has 3 times as many stickers as Anna. Dawn has 3 times as many stickers as Rosa. Sara has 17 fewer stickers than Dawn.

a How many stickers does Rosa have? Show your work.

b How many stickers does Dawn have? Show your work.

c How many stickers does Sara have? Show your work.

NAME | DATE

 Measuring in Centimeters page 1 of 3

Note to Families

This Home Connection asks students to measure common items at home in centimeters. If you have a ruler or tape measure at home marked in centimeters, have your child use it. If not, you can cut out the strips below and tape or glue them together to create a measuring tape.

Measuring in Centimeters

1 Find a ruler or tape measure that is marked in centimeters. You can also cut out the strips below and tape or glue them together to make your own measuring tape.

2 By yourself or with a family member or two, measure the items listed on the worksheet and record your results.

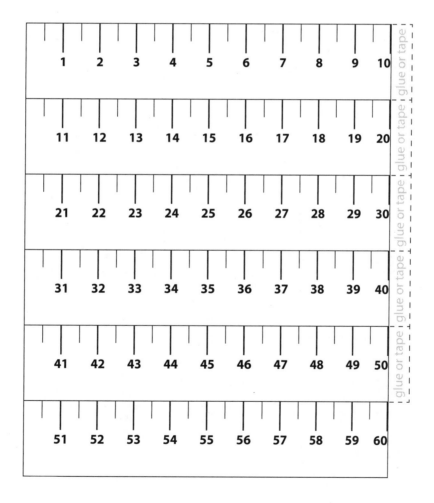

(continued on next page)

NAME _____ |DATE _____

Measuring in Centimeters page 2 of 3

Please measure the following objects in centimeters and record the results.

Object To Be Measured	Measurement in Centimeters
1 width of your bed	
2 width of a door	
3 height from the floor to the seat of your favorite chair	
4 length of a telephone or cell phone	
5 dimensions of your favorite book (length and width)	
6 width of your refrigerator	
7 dimensions of a towel (length and width)	
8 length of your toothbrush	

(continued on next page)

Measuring in Centimeters page 3 of 3

Locate objects at home that are about 6 cm and 80 cm long or tall. Record the name of the object below.

Approximate Length	Object You Found
1 about 6 cm long or tall	
2 about 80 cm long or tall	

3 Jasmine is making cookies for the fourth grade class. The recipe calls for 8 ounces of chocolate chips. She needs to triple the recipe to have enough for everyone, and she is going to add 2 more ounces of chocolate chips to the tripled batch to make the cookies extra delicious. How many ounces of chocolate chips does she need?

a Use numbers, labeled sketches, or words to solve the problem. Show your work.

b Fill in the bubble beside the equation that best represents this problem. (The letter c stands for ounces of chocolate chips.)

○ $8 + 3 + 2 = c$ ○ $(8 \times 3) + 2 = c$ ○ $(8 \times 3) - 2 = c$

4 Jasmine can fit 12 cookies on a cookie sheet. She needs 6 times that many cookies for the whole fourth grade. Jasmine also wants to have 2 cookies for each of the 4 teachers. How many cookies does Jasmine need to make? Show your work.

5 **CHALLENGE** When 2 pieces of rope are placed end-to-end, they measure 40 meters in length. When the 2 pieces are laid side-by-side, one is 10 meters longer than the other. How long is each piece of rope? Show your work.

NAME David eormmath | DATE

🏠 More Multiplying by Ten page 1 of 2

1 For each rectangle below, label the dimensions, find the area, and write an equation to describe the array.

Labeled Array	Area	Multiplication Equation
ex 10 / 6	60 sq. units	6 units × 10 units = 60 sq. units
a 10 / 8	80 sq units	8 units × 10 units = 80 sq units
b 10 / 7	70 sq units	7 units × 10 = 70 sq units
c 10 10 10 10 / 10	100 sq units	~~100 units × 10~~ 100 units × 10 = 100 sq units

(continued on next page)

More Multiplying by Ten page 2 of 2

2 Write a multiplication equation or story problem in each empty box to complete the table.

Story Problems	Multiplication Equation
ex Sarah has 5 dimes. How much money does she have?	5 × 10¢ = 50¢
a James has 12 dimes in his pocket. How much money does he have?	
b Larry had 16 dimes in his collection of old coins. How much money does he have?	
c	10¢ × 30 = $3.00
d	21 × 10¢ = $2.10

3 **CHALLENGE** Dana has only nickels in her hand, and Ajah has exactly the same number of dimes and no other coins. Together they have a total of 90¢. How many coins is each person holding? Show your work below.

NAME | DATE

🏠 Which Operation? page 1 of 3

1 Josie was planning a party. She drew a sketch of how she wanted to set up the chairs and tables. Which equation best represents the number of chairs she sketched?

○ 4 + 6 = 10   ○ 6 × 4 = 24   ○ 42 − 4 = 20   ○ 6 × 6 = 36

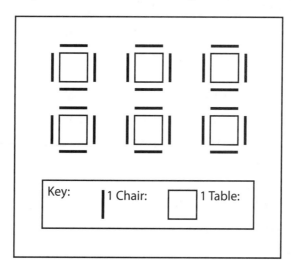

Key: |1 Chair: □ 1 Table:

2 There were 24 kids at Josie's party (including her), and each of them ate 3 pieces of pizza. Which expression shows how many pieces of pizza they ate in all?

○ 3 + 24   ○ 24 − 3   ○ 24 ÷ 3   ○ 24 × 3

3 At the end of the party, the kids broke open the piñata. When they scrambled for the candy, Gabe got 5 pieces. Maria got 3 times as many pieces as Gabe. Which of the numbers described below shows how many pieces of candy Maria got?

○ The sum of 5 and 3   ○ The difference between 5 and 3
○ The product of 5 and 3   ○ The quotient of 5 and 3

4 Josie has 5 gallons of fruit punch. This table shows how many cups there are in different numbers of gallons.

Gallons	Cups
1	16
2	32
3	48

What is one way to figure out how many cups of punch that is?

○ Add 16 to 5   ○ Multiply 5 by 16
○ Divide 16 by 5   ○ Subtract 5 from 16

(continued on next page)

NAME _____ |DATE _____

Which Operation? page 2 of 3

5 Draw a line to match each story problem below to the equation that best shows how to solve the problem. Then complete each equation. You can use the Base Ten Grid Paper on the next page if you like.

a Josie's mom bought 4 packages of mini-candy bars to put in the piñata. There were 28 in each package. How many mini-candy bars were there in all?

$28 + 4 =$ _____

b Josie got 28 napkins out of the package but then realized that she could put 4 of them away. How many did she set out on the tables?

$28 - 4 =$ _____

c Josie's brother blew up 28 balloons for the party and had enough to put 4 at each table. How many tables were there?

$28 \times 4 =$ _____

d Josie had $28 in her savings account. Josie earned $10 helping with chores. Josie spent $6 right away, but she put the other $4 in her account. How much money did she have in her savings account then?

$28 \div 4 =$ _____

6 Write a story problem for each of the two equations below, and then solve your own problems. Use the Base Ten Grid Paper on the next page if you like.

Equations	Story Problems	Solution
a $16 \times 8 =$ _____		
b $16 \div 8 =$ _____		

7 **CHALLENGE** Josie's mom bought 9 pizzas for the party. How will she need to cut them in order to have enough pieces for the party? (See Problem 2 for more information.) Use numbers, sketches, or words to show your work on another sheet of paper.

(continued on next page)

NAME | DATE

Which Operation? page 3 of 3

Base Ten Grid Paper

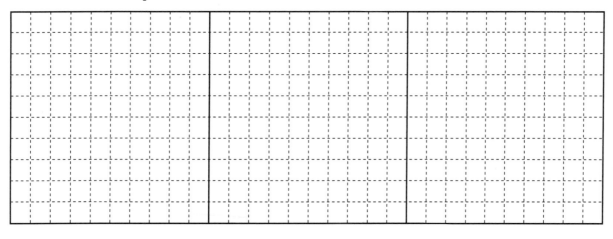

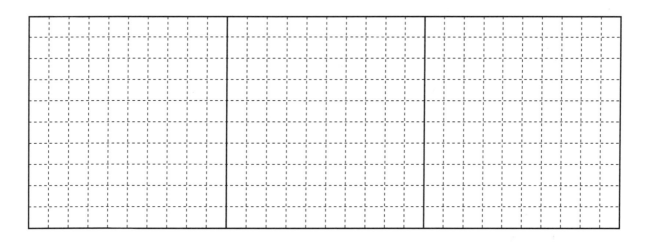

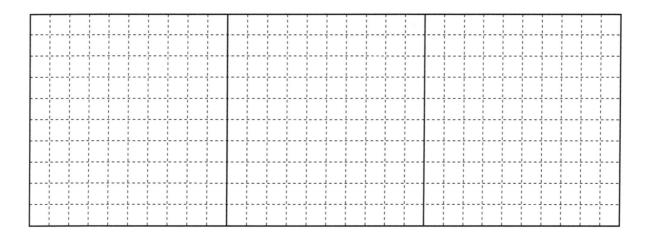

Coins & Arrays page 1 of 2

1 Write a multiplication equation to show how much each group of coins is worth.

Coin	Group of Coins		Multiplication Equation
	ex	5 nickels	$5 \times 5¢ = 25¢$
	a	10 nickels	
	b	15 nickels	
	c	10 dimes	
	d	20 dimes	
	e	30 dimes	
	f	8 quarters	
	g	12 quarters	
	h	17 quarters	

2 Label each array frame below. Then fill it in with labeled rectangles. Write an equation to show how you got the total, and then write a multiplication equation to match the array. (Cut out the base ten area pieces if you want to build the arrays.)

Labeled Array Frame & Rectangles	Addition Equation	Multiplication Equation
ex 4 ⎡ 10 ⎤ ⎡ 4 ⎤ / 4 × 10 / 4 × 4	$40 + 16 = 56$	$4 \times 14 = 56$
a		

(continued on next page)

NAME _____ | **DATE** _____

Coins & Arrays page 2 of 2

	Labeled Array Frame & Rectangles	Addition Equation	Multiplication Equation
b			
c			

3 **CHALLENGE** Raina said, "How many different ways are there to make 30¢ using pennies, nickels, dimes, or quarters?"

a What is this problem asking you to do?

b Check the strategy you plan to use (check one):

___ guess and check   ___ make a table or an organized list
___ draw a diagram   ___ other

c Show your work below.

d There are _____ different ways to make 30¢ using pennies, nickels, dimes, or quarters.

🏠 Multiplication Strategies page 1 of 2

1 Solve these problems in your head. Fill in the blanks.

10	20	30	▢	50	60	70
× 3	× 3	× 3	× 3	× 3	× 3	× 3
▢	▢	▢	120	▢	▢	▢

80	90	100	1,000	10,000	▢	1,000,000
× ▢	× 3	× 3	× 3	× 3	× 3	× 3
240	▢	▢	▢	▢	300,000	▢

2 Explain any strategies you used to make it easier to figure out the answers to the problems above.

3 Solve these problems in your head. Fill in the blanks.

10	20	30	40	50	60	70
× 4	× 5	× 7	× 2	× 5	× 4	× 5

80	90	100	1,000	60	70	80
× 4	× 5	× 8	× 9	× 8	× 2	× 5

400	300	500	600	200	700	800
× 4	× 6	× 5	× 9	× 8	× 4	× 5

(continued on next page)

Multiplication Strategies page 2 of 2

4 Look at the rectangle below. If the area is 240 square centimeters and one side is 12 centimeters, what is the length of the other side?

- Show your work.
- Write the answer on the line provided below. Be sure to label it with the correct units.

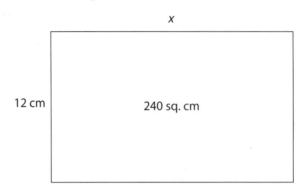

x

12 cm   240 sq. cm

The length of the side labeled x is _____

5 Sonia measured the cover of the library book she was reading. The length was 10 inches and the width was 5 inches. Which equation below represents how to find the area of her book's cover? Fill in the bubble to show.

  ○ $10 \div 5 = a$ ○ $10 - 5 = a$ ○ $10 \times 5 = a$ ○ $10 + 5 = a$

6 Fill in the ratio table for 31.

1	2	20		30	10	5	
31			93				1550

7 CHALLENGE

900	400	800	600	700	800	800
× 9	× 12	× 9	× 12	× 11	× 8	× 12

Multiplying by Multiples of Ten page 1 of 2

1 Solve each problem below:

a $2 \times 16 = 32$

b $20 \times 16 = 320$

c $4 \times 21 = 84$

d $40 \times 21 = 840$

e $8 \times 15 = 120$

f $80 \times 15 = 1200$

2 Fill in the blanks

a $6 \times 20 = 6 \times 2 \times 12$

b $30 \times 8 = 3 \times 0 \times 8$

c $5 \times 100 = 1 \times 10 \times 10$

d $40 \times 7 = 1 \times 10 \times 7$

4 Fill in the Multiple Wheel below.

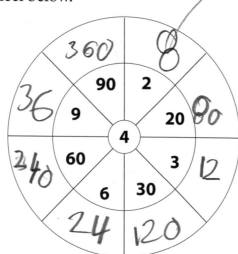

222222

(continued on next page)

Multiplying by Multiples of Ten page 2 of 2

5 Kyra is putting up streamers for a party. She uses 75 feet of streamers to decorate one wall. Two more walls also each use 75 feet of streamers. Kyra cuts 75 feet of streamers for the last wall, but this wall has a large poster on it, and she only needs to use 68 feet of streamers. How many feet of streamers did Kyra use in all?

6 **CHALLENGE** Luis and Kyra are getting ready for the party. Luis makes 6 sheets of cookies. Each sheet has 13 cookies on it. He also makes 4 trays of brownies. Each tray has 16 brownies on it. How many cookies and brownies did Luis make in all?

NAME _____ | DATE _____

 Design a Floor Pattern page 1 of 3

Note to Families
This Home Connection combines math and design. Students use their creativity to design a pattern and then practice computation to determine how much it would cost to make that pattern in tiles.

1 Choose one of the two Floor Plans: Floor Plan 1 below or Floor Plan 2 on the back of this page. (If you really enjoy this project, you can do both.)

2 Draw one of the following 3 tile designs in each square on your floor plan. Do not use the same design for every square.

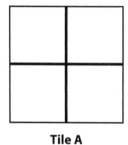   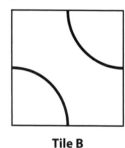   

Tile A   Tile B   Tile C

3 Answer questions 1–6 on the worksheet.

Floor Plan 1

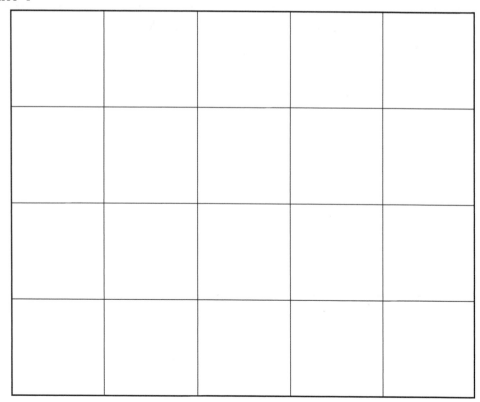

(continued on next page)

NAME | DATE

Design a Floor Pattern page 2 of 3

Floor Plan 2

(continued on next page)

38

NAME _____ | DATE _____

Design a Floor Pattern page 3 of 3

Calculating the Costs of Your Floor Pattern(s)

Here is the cost of each tile.

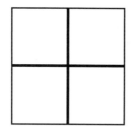

Tile A: 25 cents

Tile B: 50 cents

Tile C: 1 dollar

Use your floor plan(s) and the information above to answer the questions below (Remember, you only have to do one of the floor plans, not both.)

Question	Floor Plan 1	Floor Plan 2
1 How many tiles did you need for the floor plan you chose?		
2 How many of each tile did you use in your design of the floor plan?	**a**	**a**
	b	**b**
	c	**c**
3 How much money did all the A tiles cost?		
4 How much money did all the B tiles cost?		
5 How much money did all the C tiles cost?		
6 How much money did the entire floor pattern cost?		

| DATE

 Multiplying & Dividing page 1 of 2

1 Fill in the missing numbers.

8	6	7	6	6
× 4	× 5	× 7	× 8	× 6

8	9			8
× ▨	× ▨	× 5	× 6	× ▨
56	63	25	42	72

2 Complete the multiplication tables below.

ex

×	5	2	9	3	8	6	7	4
2	10	4	18	6	16	12	14	8

a

×	5	2	9	3	8	6	7	4
10								

b

×	5	2	9	3	8	6	7	4
5								

c

×	5	2	9	3	8	6	7	4
9								

3 Use what you know about multiplying by 10 to help solve these problems.

12	12	12	18	18	18
× 10	× 5	× 9	× 10	× 5	× 10

(continued on next page)

41

Multiplying & Dividing page 2 of 2

4 Mrs. Larsen was making gift bags for the 6 students in her reading group. She was putting little erasers in the bags. She had a bag of 20 erasers. How many erasers did each student get? Show all your work.

5 a The teacher wanted his class to work in groups of 4. After he divided them into groups, there were 6 groups of 4 and 1 group of 3. How many students were in the class? Show all your work.

b If the teacher wanted all the groups to be exactly the same size, how many students should be in each group? How many small groups would there be? Show all your work.

NAME | DATE

🏠 Multiplication & Division Puzzles page 1 of 2

1 Fill in the missing numbers.

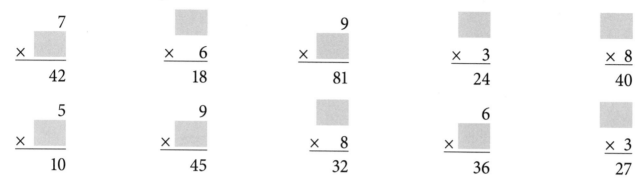

2 Use multiplication and division to find the secret path through each maze. The starting and ending points are marked for you. You can only move one space up, down, over, or diagonally each time. Write four equations to explain the path through the maze.

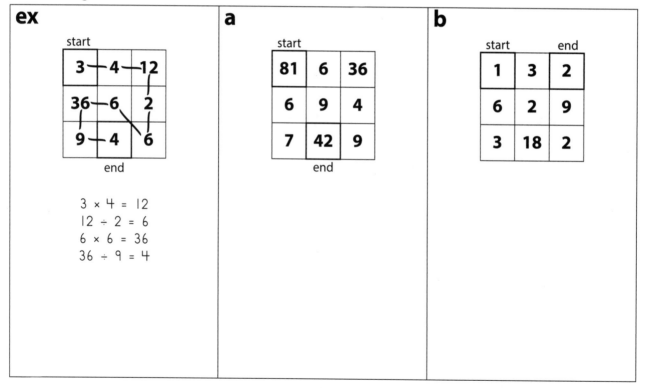

3 Complete the division table below.

÷	60	24	12	18	54	540	180	120
6								

(continued on next page)

43

NAME _____ **| DATE** _____

Multiplication & Division Puzzles page 2 of 2

4 Ryan bought 4 dozen eggs. His recipe for cookies calls for 3 eggs in each batch. How many batches of cookies can he make with the eggs he bought?

5 CHALLENGE Write a story problem to match the equation $36 \div 5 = 7 \text{ R1}$.

NAME | DATE

 Moolah on My Mind page 1 of 3

Note to Families

For this Home Connection, you'll play a game called Moolah on My Mind with your child. We have played the game in school, and your child can help you learn to play. You can also follow the directions below. The game is designed to provide practice multiplying large numbers using coin values, which are easier for many students to work with right now.

You'll need two pencils and a paperclip to play Moolah on My Mind. Use your pencil and the paperclip as a spinner.

Instructions for Moolah on My Mind

1 Take turns spinning one of the number spinners with a partner. The player with the highest number goes first.

2 Spin both number spinners and the coin spinner.

3 Write an expression in the first column to show the results of your spins. You'll add the two numbers and multiply by the value of the coin.

4 Multiply to find out how much money you collected and write that amount in the second column. Write it again in the last column so you can keep a running total of your money.

5 Take turns with your partner. Help each other make sure that you are adding your money accurately. In other words, be sure each other's running totals are correct.

6 When both players have taken 10 turns, the game is over and the player with the most money wins.

7 Play another round if you like, using the optional record sheets.

Moolah on My Mind Spinner

(continued on next page)

NAME _____ | DATE _____

Moolah on My Mind page 2 of 3

Moolah on My Mind Record Sheet

Student		
Multiplication Expression sum of the 2 numbers times the coin value	**Amount of Money You Got This Turn**	**Total So Far**
(+) × ¢		

Family Member		
Multiplication Expression sum of the 2 numbers times the coin value	**Amount of Money You Got This Turn**	**Total So Far**
(+) × ¢		

(continued on next page)

  46

Moolah on My Mind page 3 of 3

Moolah on My Mind Record Sheet (optional second game)

Student		
Multiplication Expression sum of the 2 numbers times the coin value	**Amount of Money You Got This Turn**	**Total So Far**
(+) × ¢		

Family Member		
Multiplication Expression sum of the 2 numbers times the coin value	**Amount of Money You Got This Turn**	**Total So Far**
(+) × ¢		

NAME | DATE

 Skills Review 2 page 1 of 2

1 Did you know that there are 14 Life Saver candies in a roll of Life Savers? Fill in the blanks on the ratio table to show how many Life Savers there are in different numbers of rolls.

Number of Rolls	Number of Lifesavers
1 roll	14 Life Savers
3 rolls	
	56 Life Savers
8 rolls	
	140 Life Savers

2 When people play a game of pool, they often use 15 numbered balls and 1 cue ball for a total of 16 balls. Fill in the blanks on the ratio table to show how many balls there are in different numbers of sets.

Number of Sets	Number of Balls
1 set	16 balls
2 sets	
	64 balls
5 sets	
	160 balls

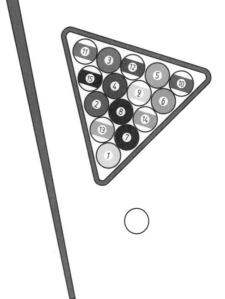

3 List all the factor pairs for the number 36.

4 List all the factor pairs for the number 42.

(continued on next page)

49

Skills Review 2 page 2 of 2

5 Bryce has a rug that is 14 decimeters by 16 decimeters. Draw a sketch of Bryce's rug. Then find the area of his rug. Show your work and label the answer with the correct units.

6 Kim's bedroom is 13 feet long and 11 feet wide. Draw a sketch of Kim's bedroom floor. Then find the area of Kim's bedroom. Show your work and label the answer with the correct units.

7 CHALLENGE Ella and Jade both ran a marathon. Ella finished in 4 hours, 6 minutes, and 13 seconds. Jade finished in 4 hours, 3 minutes, and 18 seconds. Who was faster? By how many seconds? Show your work and label the answer with the correct units.

NAME _____ | **DATE** _____

 Fraction & Division Story Problems page 1 of 2

On Tuesday, David and three friends shared a large pizza for an after-school treat. Each of the four boys ate the same amount of pizza. On Thursday, David shared 2 large pizzas with 7 friends from his soccer team. Each of the 8 team members got equal amounts.

1 Use the circles below to draw labeled models showing how much pizza David got to eat on both days.

a Tuesday's Pizza Shares

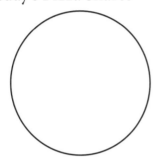

b Thursday's Pizza Shares

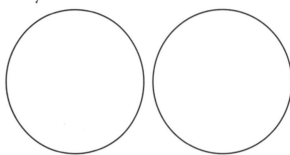

2 What fraction of a large pizza did David eat on Tuesday? _____

3 What fraction of a large pizza did David eat on Thursday? _____

4 Did David eat more pizza on Tuesday or on Thursday? _____

5 Write at least three mathematical observations that you can make from your sketches for this situation.

(continued on next page)

51

NAME _____ | **DATE** _____

Fraction & Division Story Problems page 2 of 2

6 Write a story problem to match each of the equations below:

ex $13 \div 4 = 3 \, R1$

The gym teacher has 13 playground balls for the 4 fourth grade classrooms to share. How many balls will each classroom get?

a $13 \div 4 = 3\frac{1}{4}$

b $13 \div 4 = \$3.25$

c $16 \div 4 = 4$

7 **CHALLENGE** LaToya had a large collection of basketball cards. She decided to give half of them to her friend, Erin, and a fourth of them to her brother. She still has 75 cards left. How many cards did she start with?

NAME _____ | **DATE** _____

 Thinking About Fractions page 1 of 2

1 Rico's dad brought home two pizzas that were exactly the same size. The pepperoni pizza was cut into 6 equal pieces. The cheese pizza was cut into 12 equal pieces. Rico's little brother, Luis, ate 2 pieces of pepperoni pizza. His big sister, Carlota, ate 4 pieces of the cheese pizza. Luis started crying because he thought Carlota got more pizza than he did. Carlota said they got exactly the same amount.

a Who was right, Luis or Carlota? _____

b Use labeled sketches, numbers, and words to explain your answer.

2 Vincent says that $\frac{1}{4}$ is bigger than $\frac{1}{3}$ because 4 is more than 3.

a Do you agree with Vincent? _____

b Use labeled sketches, numbers, and words to explain your answer.

(continued on next page)

53

Thinking About Fractions page 2 of 2

3 Talia says that $\frac{1}{3}$ and $\frac{2}{6}$ are equivalent fractions.

a Do you agree with Talia? _____

b Use labeled sketches, numbers, and words to explain your answer. (You can use the egg carton diagrams to help if you like.)

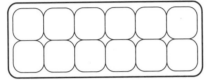 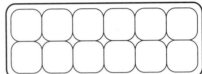

c Name another fraction that is equivalent to $\frac{1}{3}$. _____

4 **CHALLENGE** In a 12-egg carton, $\frac{1}{6}$ equals 2 eggs. Use the grids below to help you imagine and draw cartons where:

a $\frac{1}{6}$ is 3 eggs.

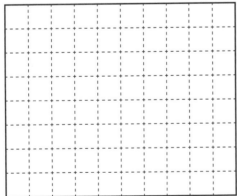

b $\frac{5}{6}$ is 25 eggs.

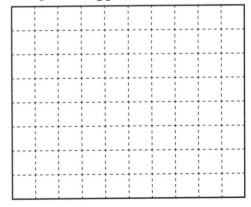

c How did you decide on the sizes of the cartons for a and b?

54

NAME _____ | DATE _____

 Brownie Dessert page 1 of 2

A fourth grade class earned a brownie dessert party for having the highest attendance in one grading period. Small pans of brownies were cut into 9 pieces, and large pans were cut into 16 pieces.

1 Tori ate 2 brownies from a small pan. What fraction of the brownies in that pan did she eat? Draw a sketch to show your thinking.

2 Holly ate 1 more brownie than Tori from the same small pan. Write two equivalent fractions that describe how much Holly ate.

3 Henry's table group seats 5 students. Each student ate 2 brownies from a large pan. Write an equation that shows what fraction of a large pan of brownies was eaten at Henry's table.

4 April ate 1 brownie from a large pan, and her friend, Christina, ate 4 brownies from the same pan.

   a Write two fractions to tell how much of the large pan of brownies Christina ate.

   b What fraction of a large pan of brownies did the girls eat together?

(continued on next page)

55

NAME | **DATE**

Brownie Dessert page 2 of 2

1 Freddy had 2 of the brownies from a large pan. His friend said he ate $\frac{1}{8}$ of the brownies in that pan. Tell why you agree or disagree.

2 **CHALLENGE** In an 18-egg carton, $\frac{1}{3}$ equals 6 eggs. Use the grids below to help you imagine and draw cartons where:

a $\frac{1}{2}$ is 9 eggs.

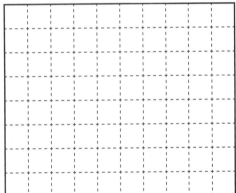

b $\frac{3}{8}$ is 18 eggs.

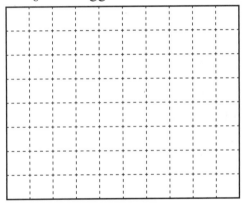

56

Planning a Garden page 1 of 2

The Brown family is trying to decide how to plan their garden for the vegetables they want to grow. Use the geoboard model to design a garden that fits each description. Label every area to show where each vegetable will be planted.

1 The Browns could plant $\frac{1}{2}$ tomatoes, $\frac{1}{4}$ squash, and $\frac{1}{4}$ lettuce.

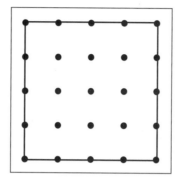

2 They could plant $\frac{1}{4}$ tomatoes, $\frac{1}{4}$ squash, $\frac{1}{4}$ lettuce, $\frac{1}{8}$ peppers, and $\frac{1}{8}$ cabbage.

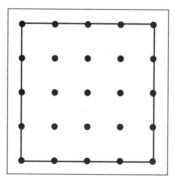

3 The Brown family might plant $\frac{1}{8}$ tomatoes, $\frac{1}{8}$ cabbage, and $\frac{1}{8}$ peppers. If they do, what fraction of their garden will be unplanted?

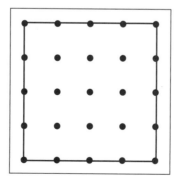

(continued on next page)

57

Planning a Garden page 2 of 2

1 If the Browns plant $\frac{3}{16}$ tomatoes, $\frac{1}{4}$ cabbage, and $\frac{2}{8}$ peppers, what fraction of their garden will be unplanted?

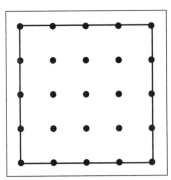

2 **CHALLENGE** Create a plan for a garden that has room for 5 different vegetables. Label the vegetables in the garden and write a equation to represent the model.

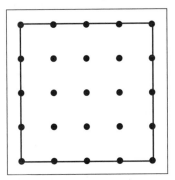

NAME _____ | DATE _____

🏠 Fractions & More Fractions page 1 of 2

1 Ethan used an egg carton model to add fractions. Draw eggs in the cartons to show and solve the problem. Then fill in the blank to show the answer.

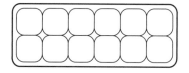 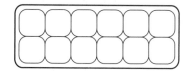 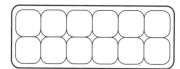

$$\frac{1}{2} \qquad + \qquad \frac{1}{6} =$$

2 Put the following numbers in order on the number line below.

$\frac{1}{2} \qquad 1\frac{1}{2} \qquad \frac{3}{5} \qquad \frac{1}{4} \qquad 1\frac{3}{4} \qquad 1\frac{1}{4} \qquad \frac{7}{8}$

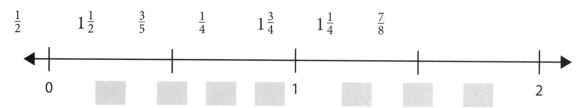

3 Maria is writing as many different addition and multiplication equations as she can for $2\frac{2}{8}$. Her rule is that all the fractions in each equation must have a denominator of 8.

a Here are the equations Maria has written so for. Fill in the bubble beside each equation that is true.

◯ $2\frac{2}{8} = 1 + 1 + \frac{2}{8}$

◯ $2\frac{2}{8} = \frac{8}{8} + \frac{10}{8}$

◯ $\frac{5}{8} + \frac{5}{8} + \frac{5}{8} + \frac{4}{8} = 2\frac{2}{8}$

◯ $18 \times \frac{1}{8} = 2\frac{2}{8}$

b Write at least four more addition or multiplication equations for $2\frac{2}{8}$ in which all the fractions have a denominator of 8.

(continued on next page)

59

Fractions & More Fractions page 2 of 2

4 Calvin and Leah are playing a game that has them draw fraction cards to add up to numbers that fill a 12-egg carton. Calvin had $\frac{1}{3}$ of his egg carton full when he chose a card with $\frac{8}{12}$ on it. He says he will fill his egg carton. Do you agree or disagree? Why? Use a labeled sketch in the egg carton diagram below to help explain your answer.

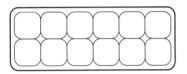

5 Leah had $\frac{4}{6}$ of her egg carton full when she chose the $\frac{5}{12}$ card. Can she fit $\frac{5}{12}$ in this egg carton? Why or why not? Use a labeled sketch in the egg carton diagram below to help explain your answer.

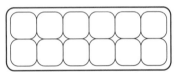

6 **CHALLENGE** Imagine you are playing the game with egg cartons that hold 18 eggs, and the fraction cards refer to 18 eggs instead of 12 eggs. (For example, if you draw the $\frac{1}{2}$ card, that means half of 18, not half of 12.)

a If you have $\frac{2}{3}$ of your first 18-egg carton full, how many more eggs will fit in that carton? What fraction card will you need to draw to fill the first carton exactly?

b You have $\frac{1}{3}$ of your second 18-egg carton full when you select the $\frac{5}{6}$ card. Can you use this card to place more eggs in the second carton, or will you have to use your third carton instead?

NAME _____ | DATE _____

🏠 More Comparing Decimals & Fractions page 1 of 2

1 Which fraction is larger: $\frac{8}{10}$ or $\frac{73}{100}$?

   a Explain why you think so.

   b Draw each fraction on a grid below to verify your answer.

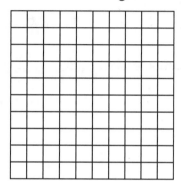 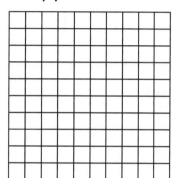

   c Record each fraction as a decimal number.

     $\frac{8}{10}$ _____ $\frac{73}{100}$ _____

2 On the first grid below, shade a number between 0.75 and 0.8 and label it. Then shade in and label a different number between 0.75 and 0.8 on the second grid.

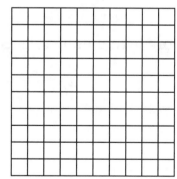 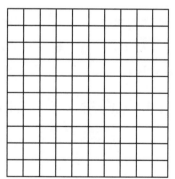

   _____   _____

   a Compare the two numbers you shaded in the grids. Write an inequality using the symbol < or > to show which number is larger.

(continued on next page)

More Comparing Decimals & Fractions page 2 of 2

3 Write these numbers as decimals:

a Two and eighty-three hundredths _____

b One and six hundredths _____

4 Write this decimal number in words: 2.94.

5 Fill in each blank with <, >, or =.

a 0.8 _____ 0.78   **b** 0.56 _____ 0.6   **c** 0.6 _____ 0.60

6 Allison says that 1.06 is bigger than 1.2 because 6 is bigger than 2. Do you agree or disagree? Explain.

7 Erik is 4.23 feet tall. Stacy is 4.3 feet tall. Who is taller? Explain.

8 **CHALLENGE** One year ago, Charlie's chameleon was 8.42 inches long. Now his chameleon is 9.36 inches long. Show your work with numbers, labeled sketches, or words for each question below.

a How much did Charlie's chameleon grow in the last year?

b How much more does his chameleon need to grow to be exactly 10 inches?

NAME _____ | DATE _____

🏠 Decimals, Fractions & Story Problems page 1 of 2

1 Write the place value of the underlined digit in each number. The place values are spelled correctly for you here:

hundreds   tens   ones   tenths   hundredths

ex 2.0<u>3</u> hundredths	**a** 3.<u>1</u>7
b 12<u>0</u>.4	**c** <u>5</u>06.92
d 54.2<u>9</u>	**e** 32.<u>7</u>

2 Write each decimal number.

> **ex** Twenty-three and two-tenths: __23.2__

> **ex** One hundred thirty and five-hundredths: __130.05__

a Six and seven-hundredths: _____

b Two-hundred sixty-five and eight-tenths: _____

3 Write each fraction or mixed number as a decimal number.

ex $5\frac{3}{10}$ 5.3	**ex** $12\frac{4}{100}$ 12.04	**ex** $3\frac{17}{100}$ 3.17
a $\frac{7}{10}$	**b** $3\frac{5}{100}$	**c** $\frac{4}{100}$
d $4\frac{38}{100}$	**e** $1\frac{9}{100}$	**f** $1\frac{9}{10}$

4 Use a greater than (>), less than (<), or equal sign to show the relationship between the decimal numbers below.

ex 1.09 < 1.9	**a** 1.12 ___ 1.2	**b** 3.5 ___ 3.48
c 23.81 ___ 23.85	**d** 4.50 ___ 4.5	**e** 3.06 ___ 3.65

(continued on next page)

NAME _____ | DATE _____

Decimals, Fractions & Story Problems page 2 of 2

5 Write two fractions to show what part of each mat has been shaded in—one with denominator 10 and an equivalent fraction with denominator 100.

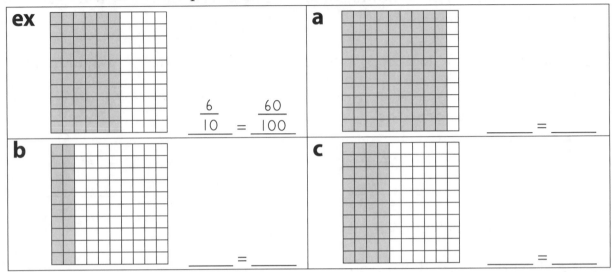

ex $\frac{6}{10} = \frac{60}{100}$

a ____ = ____

b ____ = ____

c ____ = ____

6 Last Friday, Ray went home with his cousin Jewel after school. They took the city bus to Jewel's house. It costs $1.65 to ride the bus. Ray had 5 quarters, a dime, and 3 nickels. How much more money did he need to ride the bus? Show all your work.

a How much did it cost Ray and Jewel to ride the bus in all? Show all your work.

7 Ray's school is 1.7 miles from his house. He walks to and from school every day. How many miles does he walk each day? Show all your work.

a **CHALLENGE** How many miles does he walk in a 5-day school week? Show all your work.

Equal, Not Equal page 1 of 2

1 Fill in the bubble to show the equation that is correct.

○ $1\frac{1}{4} + 1\frac{1}{4} = 2\frac{3}{4}$ ○ $5\frac{2}{8} - 3\frac{1}{8} = 2\frac{3}{8}$

○ $4\frac{3}{12} + 2\frac{9}{12} = 6\frac{11}{12}$ ○ $\frac{3}{10} + \frac{32}{100} = \frac{62}{100}$

2 Fill in the bubble to show the equation that is *not* correct.

○ $\frac{6}{10} + \frac{15}{100} = \frac{75}{100}$ ○ $\frac{7}{8} - \frac{3}{8} = \frac{1}{3}$

○ $\frac{5}{12} + \frac{7}{12} = \frac{12}{12}$ ○ $\frac{10}{12} - \frac{4}{12} = \frac{1}{2}$

3 Fill in the bubbles to show the comparison statements that are correct. (There is more than one.)

○ $0.3 < 0.03$ ○ $\frac{2}{8} = \frac{1}{4}$

○ $0.6 > 0.49$ ○ $0.7 = 0.70$

4 Fill in the bubbles to show the comparison statements that are *not* correct. (There is more than one.)

○ $0.05 = \frac{1}{2}$ ○ $0.25 > 0.3$

○ $0.4 = \frac{60}{100}$ ○ $\frac{6}{10} < \frac{60}{100}$

5 Put the fractions and decimal numbers in the correct places on the number line:

0.75   1.5 $\frac{1}{4}$ $1\frac{3}{4}$ $\frac{3}{8}$ $1\frac{1}{4}$

(continued on next page)

Equal, Not Equal page 2 of 2

6 Fill in the table below with a base ten model, decimal, or fraction. The first one has been done for you.

Base Ten Model	Decimal	Fraction
	0.25	$\frac{25}{100}$ or $\frac{1}{4}$
	0.75	

Base Ten Model	Decimal	Fraction
		$\frac{6}{10}$

7 Daniel collects baseball cards and keeps them in a special binder. Each page holds 9 baseball cards in a 3 × 3 array. The first page is $\frac{4}{9}$ full. The second page is $\frac{1}{3}$ full. If Daniel put all the cards onto just one page, what fraction of that page would be full? Use numbers, labeled sketches, or words to model and solve the problem.

8 **CHALLENGE** Sienna also collects baseball cards in a binder just like Daniel's. Her last page was $\frac{6}{9}$ full, but she gave $\frac{1}{3}$ of those cards to Daniel.

a What fraction of Sienna's last page is full now? Use numbers, labeled sketches, or words to model and solve the problem.

b Can Daniel fit the cards from his first page, his second page, and the cards Sienna gave him all on one page in his binder? Use labeled sketches, numbers or words to show your thinking.

66

NAME _____ | **DATE** _____

 Frankie's Fractions & Decimals page 1 of 2

Solve the following problems. Use numbers, words, or labeled sketches to show your thinking.

1 Frankie's dad made scrambled eggs for the family's breakfast. He started with a full carton of 12 eggs. He used 8 of the eggs. What fraction of the carton of eggs did he use? Write at least two equivalent fractions.

2 Frankie found a quarter on the sidewalk.

a What fraction of a dollar did Frankie find? Write at least two equivalent fractions.

b Write the amount of money Frankie found as a decimal. _____

3 Frankie ate $\frac{3}{8}$ of a granola bar. Her friend Pablo ate $\frac{4}{8}$ of the granola bar.

a What fraction of the granola bar did they eat in all?

b How much of the granola bar is left?

4 Write each fraction as an equivalent fraction with 100 in the denominator.

ex $\frac{4}{10} = \frac{40}{100}$　　$\frac{2}{10} =$ _____　　　$\frac{6}{10} =$ _____　　　$\frac{9}{10} =$ _____　　　$\frac{5}{10} =$ _____

5 Add or subtract.

a $1\frac{2}{4} + 3\frac{2}{4} =$ _____　　**b** $\frac{1}{5} +$ _____ $= \frac{3}{5}$　　**c** $\frac{4}{10} + \frac{23}{100} =$ _____

d $\frac{50}{100} - \frac{2}{10} =$ _____　　**e** $\frac{10}{12} -$ _____ $= \frac{4}{12}$　　**f** $\frac{75}{100} - \frac{5}{10} =$ _____

(continued on next page)

Frankie's Fractions & Decimals page 2 of 2

6 Frankie wrote this equation on her paper during math class: $1\frac{2}{3} = \frac{3}{3} + \frac{2}{3}$.

a Is Frankie's equation true?_____

b Write three more equations for $1\frac{2}{3}$ that are all true and all different. Use only fractions with a denominator of 3 in your equations.

$1\frac{2}{3} = $ _____

$1\frac{2}{3} = $ _____

$1\frac{2}{3} = $ _____

7 Frankie's teacher asked each of the students to cut a square of grid paper any size they wanted. Frankie cut out a 10 × 10 grid, and her friend Lori cut out an 8 × 8 grid. Then the teacher said, "Each grid you cut, no matter what size, has a value of 1. Please shade in exactly $\frac{1}{4}$ of your grid."

a Here are the grids Frankie and Lori cut out. Shade in exactly $\frac{1}{4}$ of each grid.

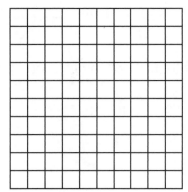   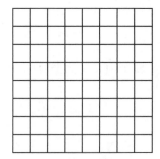

Frankie's 10 × 10 grid   Lori's 8 × 8 grid

b How many little squares did you shade in on Frankie's grid? _____

How many little squares did you shade in on Lori's grid? _____

c Why did you need to shade in a different number of squares on each grid, even though you shaded in one-fourth on both of them?

NAME David carmarath | DATE

 Number Riddles & Stories page 1 of 2

1 Draw a line to show which number matches each description. The first one is done for you.

ex This number has a 2 in the thousands place.   46,305

a This is an even number with a 6 in the hundreds place.   32,617

b This number is equal to 30,000 + 4,000 + 80 + 2.   45,052

c This number is 1,000 less than 46,052.   19,628

d This is an odd number with a 6 in the thousands place.   34,082

2 Write each number in words.

ex	17,329	seventeen thousand, three hundred twenty-nine
a	33,072	thirte three thousand, Sevende two
b	86,105	eightu six thousand one hundred five
c	74,629	Sevende four thousand six hundred twenty nine

3 **CHALLENGE** Write an even number that has a 7 in the hundreds place, has an odd number in the thousands place, and is a multiple of 10.

(continued on next page)

| DATE

Number Riddles & Stories page 2 of 2

Solve the problems below. Show all your work.

4 Felipe's family is driving to see his grandmother. Altogether, they have to drive 856 miles. If they have gone 269 miles so far, how much farther do they have to drive?

5 In our classroom library, we had 326 books. We gave 38 books to the other fourth grade classroom, but our teacher got 97 more books for our classroom library. How many books do we have in our classroom library now?

6 **CHALLENGE** At the school fair, students were guessing how many jellybeans were in a jar. Nicky guessed there were 296 jellybeans. Caitlyn guessed there were 435 jellybeans. Samira guessed a number that was 52 more than Nicky and Caitlyn's put together. What was Samira's guess?

70

NAME David carmonchp | DATE

 Big Numbers page 1 of 2

1 Each weekend, Dylan and his dad go fishing. Dylan checks the odometer reading before each trip and records it in their mileage book. (An odometer is an instrument on the dashboard of a car that tells how far you've driven in all.) Put these readings in the order that they would appear in the book, from least to greatest. The first one has been done for you.

93,102   90,089   89,776   91,438   95,004   99,173   91,204

2 Look at the following numbers. Circle the number that is the closest to 60,034.

60,000   60,100   60,200   60,300

3 Circle the number closest to 194,321.

190,000   191,000   192,000   193,000   194,000   195,000   196,000

4 Circle the number closest to 233,904.

230,000   231,000   232,000   233,000   234,000   235,000   135,000

5 Circle the number closest to 234,900,032.

232,000,000   233,000,000   234,000,000   235,000,000

(continued on next page)

NAME _____ | DATE _____

Big Numbers page 2 of 2

6 Round each of the numbers below to the nearest hundred. Use the number line to help if you like. (Hint: Look at the number in the tens place.)

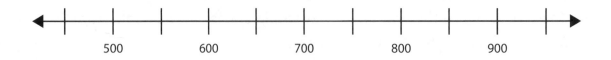

500 600 700 800 900

567 rounds to _____   717 rounds to _____   889 rounds to _____

450 rounds to _____   649 rounds to _____   905 rounds to _____

7 Round each of the numbers below to the nearest 1,000. Use the number line to help if you like. (Hint: Look at the number in the hundreds place.)

5,000 6,000 7,000 8,000 9,000

4,903 rounds to _____   5,099 rounds to _____   9,499 rounds to _____

7,500 rounds to _____   8,750 rounds to _____   6,138 rounds to _____

8 Amanda is sure she got the high score on a video game, but she's not sure what the number is.

a Please write it down for her using base ten numbers. She scored nine hundred forty-three million, two hundred sixty-one thousand, five hundred eighty-six.

b Caleb is positive he beat Amanda's score. His score was 925,298,199. Who got the higher score? How do you know?

NAME _____ | **DATE** _____

 Addition Algorithm & More page 1 of 2

1 Solve the problems below using the standard algorithm for addition.

$$\begin{array}{r} 157 \\ +\ 188 \\ \hline \end{array} \qquad \begin{array}{r} 252 \\ +\ 679 \\ \hline \end{array} \qquad \begin{array}{r} 399 \\ +\ 411 \\ \hline \end{array} \qquad \begin{array}{r} 676 \\ +\ 297 \\ \hline \end{array}$$

2 Alonzo used the standard algorithm to solve the problem below.

$$\begin{array}{r} {\scriptstyle 1} \\ 176 \\ +\ 258 \\ \hline 324 \end{array}$$

a Did Alonzo use the algorithm correctly? Explain your answer.

b How would you solve 176 + 258? Show your work.

3 Patricia used the standard algorithm to solve the problem below.

$$\begin{array}{r} {\scriptstyle 6\,3} \\ 384 \\ +\ 559 \\ \hline 1411 \end{array}$$

a Did Patricia use the algorithm correctly? Explain your answer.

b How would you solve 384 + 559? Show your work.

(continued on next page)

Addition Algorithm & More page 2 of 2

Review

4 Fill in the blanks in the multiple wheel below.

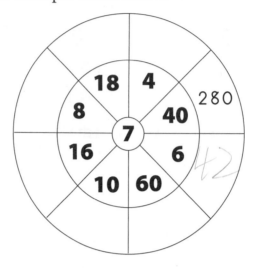

5 Fill in the blanks in the equations below.

$5 \times 20 = 5 \times 2 \times$ _____ $12 \times 30 = 12 \times$ _____ $\times 10$ $8 \times$ _____ $= 8 \times 6 \times 10$

6 Simon wants to add 3 numbers that total 1,000. He starts with these numbers: 567 and 354.

a What is the sum of Simon's first two addends? Show your work.

b What number does Simon need to reach 1,000? Show your work.

7 **CHALLENGE** Isabella babysits so she can earn money for a new snowboard. She charges $6.75 an hour. In April, Isabella babysat for 10 hours on one weekend, 12 hours another weekend, and 20 hours during another weekend. How much money did Isabella earn babysitting in April?

Think Before You Add page 1 of 2

1 Study each problem before you begin to solve it. Think about which strategy would
be most efficient (easiest and fastest). Choose your strategy and solve the problem.
Use the space below the problems if you need it to do your figuring.

$$
\begin{array}{r} 99 \\ +\ 43 \\ \hline 142 \end{array}
\qquad
\begin{array}{r} 878 \\ +121 \\ \hline 999 \end{array}
\qquad
\begin{array}{r} 213 \\ +762 \\ \hline 975 \end{array}
\qquad
\begin{array}{r} 232 \\ +75 \\ \hline 307 \end{array}
$$

2 Use the standard algorithm for addition to solve the problems below.

$$
\begin{array}{r} 189 \\ +\ 215 \\ \hline 404 \end{array}
\qquad
\begin{array}{r} 57 \\ +84 \\ \hline 141 \end{array}
\qquad
\begin{array}{r} 378 \\ +497 \\ \hline 875 \end{array}
\qquad
\begin{array}{r} 764 \\ +135 \\ \hline 899 \end{array}
$$

3 Look at the problems in item 2. Find a problem that might have been solved faster
with another strategy.

this one

a Which problem did you choose?

378
+497

$378 + 49 > 875$

$$
\begin{array}{r} +4,97 \\ \hline 875 \end{array}
$$

b Which strategy could be faster? Why?

this one is easier
for me because it go
it better than
eney other problem

(continued on next page)

Think Before You Add page 2 of 2

Mixed Review

4 Use the symbols >, =, or < to compare each pair of fractions.

ex $\frac{1}{3}$ **>** $\frac{1}{4}$ **a** $\frac{3}{6}$ **>** $\frac{2}{3}$ **b** $\frac{1}{3}$ **<** $\frac{1}{4}$ **c** $\frac{3}{4}$ **<** $\frac{5}{6}$

d $\frac{2}{3}$ **<** $\frac{3}{4}$ **e** $\frac{1}{2}$ **<** $\frac{2}{4}$ **f** $\frac{1}{3}$ **<** $\frac{2}{4}$ **g** $\frac{2}{6}$ **>** $\frac{1}{3}$

5 Write the decimal name for each fraction.

a $5\frac{9}{10} =$ 9.00   **b** $6\frac{5}{100} =$ 5.00   **c** $2\frac{6}{10} =$ 6.20   **d** $8\frac{1}{10} =$ 10.00

e $1\frac{20}{100} =$ 20.000   **f** $3\frac{4}{10} =$ 4.000   **g** $9\frac{50}{100} =$ 50.00

6 **CHALLENGE** Last year, Monica's snake was 9.62 inches long. Now her snake is 12.37 inches long. Show your work with numbers, labeled sketches, or words for each question below.

a How much did Monica's snake grow in the last year?

b How much more does her snake need to grow to be exactly 13 inches?

Number Cards page 1 of 2

Hayley pulled 6 cards from a regular deck of cards. She arranged the cards into these 3-digit numbers: 348 and 956.

1 What is the sum of Hayley's numbers? Use the strategy of your choice and show your work below.

2 What is the difference between Hayley's numbers? Use the strategy of your choice and show your work below.

3 What is the largest 6-digit number Hayley can make with the numbers she chose?

4 What is the smallest 6-digit number Hayley can make with the numbers she chose?

5 Hayley chose 6 more cards. This time she made these numbers: 278 and 421. Hayley says she can add 299 and 400 and get the same sum as 278 and 421. Do you agree or disagree? Why?

6 Hayley says she can find the difference between 278 and 421 by finding the difference between 300 and 443. Do you agree or disagree? Why?

(continued on next page)

Number Cards page 2 of 2

Review

7 Add these pairs of fractions. Express the answer for each as a fraction with denominator 100.

$\frac{5}{10} + \frac{37}{100} =$ $\frac{6}{10} + \frac{6}{100} =$ $\frac{13}{10} + \frac{87}{100} =$ $\frac{4}{10} + \frac{12}{100} =$

8 Place the decimals in their correct places on the number line.

0.4   0.1   0.8   0.25   0.55   0.95

Story Problems

9 There are 137 third graders, 139 fourth graders, and 153 fifth graders at Wood Upper Primary School. How many students are there in all? Show your work using numbers, sketches, or words.

10 CHALLENGE Sarah, Rex, and Peter are all friends. One of them lives in a red house, one lives in a blue house, and the other lives in a green house. The person who lives in a green house has more than 3 letters in his name. The person who lives in a red house is not Rex. Which person lives in each house?

🏠 Thinking About Subtraction page 1 of 2

1 Look at each subtraction problem below. Think about which strategy makes the most sense for each problem. Solve each problem.

a $\begin{array}{r} 4875 \\ -\ 4859 \\ \hline \end{array}$	What strategy did you use? Why did you use this strategy?

b $\begin{array}{r} 1{,}685 \\ -\ 1{,}685 \\ \hline \end{array}$	What strategy did you use? Why did you use this strategy?

c $\begin{array}{r} 699 \\ -\ 424 \\ \hline \end{array}$	What strategy did you use? Why did you use this strategy?

2 Fill in the blanks in the equations below.

$498 - 323 = 500 - \underline{\quad}$ $68 - \underline{\quad} = 70 - 55$ $1003 - 498 = \underline{\quad} - 495$

(continued on next page)

79

Thinking About Subtraction page 2 of 2

Review

3 Jenny got a box of 15 stickers for her birthday. Use this information as you solve each problem below. Use numbers, labeled sketches, or words to show your thinking.

a Jenny used 5 stickers on a thank-you card. What fraction of the box did she use?

b Jenny gave her brother 4 stickers. What fraction does she have left out of her box of 15?

4 After she gave some stickers to her brother, Jenny's dog ate 3 of her stickers.

a Now what fraction does Jenny have left of her original box of 15 stickers?

b What fraction of the stickers went to Jenny's brother and her dog?

5 The third grade gymnastics team has 279 points. In order to place in the top three teams, they'll need a score of 425 or more. How many more points do they need to earn in order to rank in the top three?

6 **CHALLENGE** Brendan needs to mail a 12-page letter to his friend in Texas. It costs $1.38 to mail all 12 sheets together. A 6-page letter costs 68¢ to mail. A 4-page letter costs 45¢ to mail. Envelopes costs 3¢ each. What is the least expensive way to mail his 12 pages?

NAME | DATE

🏠 Which Measurement Is Best? page 1 of 2

1 What is the best estimate of the height of the ceiling?

○ 10 inches

○ 10 feet

○ 10 meters

○ 10 centimeters

2 The length of a mouse is best measured in what units?

○ feet

○ ounces

○ centimeters

○ yards

3 What is the best estimate of the distance across your classroom?

○ 30 meters

○ 30 yards

○ 30 feet

○ 30 kilometers

4 Which of these units would best measure the length of a ladybug?

○ millimeters

○ inches

○ grams

○ feet

5 Which of these units would best measure the length of a pair of scissors?

○ grams

○ ounces

○ feet

○ centimeters

(continued on next page)

81

NAME _____ | DATE _____

Which Measurement Is Best? page 2 of 2

6 The distance across the state in which you live is best measured in what units?

○ yards

○ gallons

○ ounces

○ miles

7 Kim was using a give and take strategy. Fill in the blanks to make the equation true.

999 + 587 = 1,000 + _____ = _____

8 Kevin was using the constant difference strategy. Fill in the blanks to make the equation true.

1,256 – 799 = _____ – 800 = _____

9 **CHALLENGE** Owen had three different kinds of stickers that he wanted to put on paper. He put a bird sticker on every 30th paper, a sports sticker on every 50th paper and a robot sticker on every 60th paper. Will any of the first 600 pages have all three stickers? If so, which pages?

Running the Race page 1 of 2

Use an open number line to model and solve problems 1 and 2.

1 Anna started a race at 9:30 am. She ran for 3 hours and 47 minutes. What time did she finish her race?

2 Michael and Tyler both ran a half marathon. Michael finished in 1 hour 42 minutes and 13 seconds. Tyler finished in 97 minutes and 49 seconds.

a Who was faster?

b How much faster was he?

3 Takumi ran the first mile of his race in 450 seconds. How many minutes was his first mile?

4 Johanna used tiles to build a rectangular array with an area of 54. List all the possible dimensions of the array.

(continued on next page)

NAME _____ | DATE _____

Running the Race page 2 of 2

5 What is 329,456 rounded to the

nearest ten? _____

nearest hundred? _____

nearest thousand? _____

6 Fill in the bubble to show which number listed below is closer to 445,890:

○ 450,000

○ 440,000

7 If you wanted to round 373,417 to the nearest ten thousand, which number below would you choose?

○ 380,000

○ 370,000

8 CHALLENGE Linda plans to sign up for three Field Day events. She wants to run a total of more than a kilometer but less than 1.5 kilometers. Which three events should she sign up for? Her choices are:

Dash	Hurdles	Run
100 meter dash	200 meter hurdles	800 meter run
200 meter dash	300 meter hurdles	1600 meter run
400 meter dash		

NAME _____ | **DATE** _____

🏠 Unit 4 Review 1 page 1 of 2

1 Solve the addition problems below. Use the standard algorithm. The first one is done for you.

```
  1 1
  459          387          609         1,589
+ 144        + 414        + 734       + 3,437
─────
  603
```

2 Solve the subtraction problems below. Use the standard algorithm. The first one is done for you.

```
  7 12
  8̸3̸3          745          905         3,581
- 547        - 548        - 237       - 1,346
─────
  286
```

3 Complete each equation by writing a number in base ten numerals.

ex $\underline{17,508} = 10,000 + 7,000 + 500 + 8$ **a** $\underline{\quad\quad} = 20,000 + 400 + 50 + 6$

b $\underline{\quad\quad} = 30,000 + 2,000 + 100 + 10 + 2$ **c** $\underline{\quad\quad} = 7,000 + 40 + 6$

d $\underline{\quad\quad} = 90,000 + 6,000 + 30 + 5$ **e** $\underline{\quad\quad} = 60,000 + 3,000 + 7$

f $\underline{\quad\quad} = 10,000 + 3,000 + 800 + 50 + 5$ **g** $\underline{\quad\quad} = 50,000 + 300 + 5$

4 Fill in the missing number in each equation.

ex $40,000 + 6,000 + \underline{50} + 8 = 46,058$ **a** $41,092 = 40,000 + \underline{\quad} + 90 + 2$

b $50,000 + 1,000 + \underline{\quad} + 50 + 4 = 51,354$ **c** $17,035 = 10,000 + \underline{\quad} + 30 + 5$

d $96,035 = 90,000 + 6,000 + \underline{\quad} + 5$ **e** $20,000 + \underline{\quad} + 50 + 6 = 20,456$

f $2,000 + 500 + \underline{\quad} + 7 = 2,567$ **g** $20,408 = 20,000 + \underline{\quad} + 8$

(continued on next page)

Unit 4 Review 1 page 2 of 2

Solve the problems below. Use the standard algorithms for addition and subtraction. Show all your work.

5 In December, the cafeteria served 972 breakfast sandwiches. During the first week in January, they served 486 breakfast sandwiches. During the second week of January they served 538 breakfast sandwiches. How many more breakfast sandwiches did they serve serve in the first two weeks of January than during the whole month of December?

6 There were 6,742 bags of potato chips stored in the cafeteria. They served 781 of them at lunch and 89 more of them as snacks for the students in after-care. How many bags of potato chips are left?

7 At the basketball game last night, the home team was losing by 48 points at halftime, so fans started to leave. There were 45,862 people at the game when it started and 17,946 left at halftime. Then another 13,892 people left before the last quarter. How many people were left by the end of the game?

86

Unit 4 Review 2 page 1 of 2

The table below shows the populations of Austin, Chicago, New York City, Philadelphia, and San Francisco in the year 2010.

Population in the year 2010	
City Name	**Population**
Austin	790,390
Chicago	2,695,598
New York City	8,175,133
Philadelphia	1,526,006
San Francisco	805,235

1 Use the symbol >, =, or < to compare the populations of New York City and Philadelphia.

2 Write the population of Chicago in words.

3 The city of Denver, Colorado, had a population of six hundred thousand, one hundred fifty-eight in the year 2010. Write the population of Denver in numbers.

4 Seattle had a population of 608,660 in the year 2010. Round Seattle's population to the nearest:

a ten: _____

b hundred: _____

c thousand: _____

d Fill in the bubble to show what 608,660 would be rounded to the nearest ten thousand.

○ 600,000

○ 610,000

○ 600,900

(continued on next page)

Unit 4 Review 2 page 2 of 2

5 How many hundreds are in 1,000? _____

6 How many hundreds are in 7,000? _____

7 How many hundreds are in 10,000? _____

8 How many thousands are in 38,000? _____

9 How many ten thousands are in 200,000? _____

10 How many hundred thousands are in 5,000,000? _____

11 Fill in the blank with the correct relational symbol: <, > or =.

a 18 km _____ 20,000 meters

b 1700 grams _____ 17 kg

c $13\frac{1}{2}$ liters _____ 13,500 milliliters

12 During his practice this month, Jeff ran one 10K in 1:01:49 and another in 57: 53. How much faster was his second 10K practice? Show all your work. (Hint: Use an open number line to model and solve this problem.)

13 Alex bought a 6-pack of sports drink bottles that each had a volume of 350 ml.

a If Alex drank 3 of them, how many milliliters did she drink? Show your work.

Answer: _____ milliliters

b How many more milliliters would Alex need to drink to have 2 liters? Show your work.

Answer: _____ milliliters

NAME David Camorajt | DATE

 Reviewing Area & Perimeter page 1 of 2

1 Find the area and perimeter of each rectangle. Area is the total amount of space covered by the rectangle. Perimeter is the distance around the rectangle.

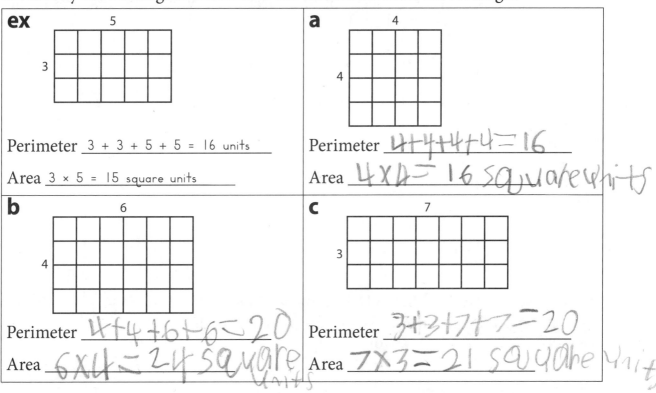

ex

5
3

Perimeter 3 + 3 + 5 + 5 = 16 units

Area 3 × 5 = 15 square units

a

4
4

Perimeter 4+4+4+4=16

Area 4×4= 16 square units

b

6
4

Perimeter 4+4+6+6=20

Area 6×4= 24 square units

c

7
3

Perimeter 3+3+7+7=20

Area 7×3= 21 square units

2 **CHALLENGE** Find the area and perimeter of this shape. Show all your work.

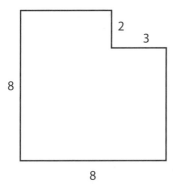

2
3
8
8

Perimeter 2+2+3+3+8+8+8+8=42

Area 2×3×8×8=70
6 64

(continued on next page)

89

Reviewing Area & Perimeter page 2 of 2

3 You can make sketches to help solve the problems below. Remember to include the units of measurement in your answers. Show all of your work.

a The classroom rug is 9 feet long and 8 feet wide. What is the total area of the rug?

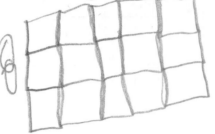

b What is the perimeter of the rug?

$8 + 8 + 9 + 9 = 34$

4 Chrissy is going to make a big painting on a piece of wood that is 4 feet wide and 7 feet long. What is the total area of the piece of wood?

a What is the perimeter of the piece of wood?

$7 + 7 + 4 + 4 = 22$

5 The school playground measures 465 feet by 285 feet. What is the perimeter of the playground?

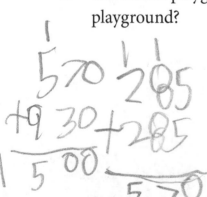

570   285   285
+930 +285
15 00 570

465   930
+465 +570
930   1500

Angles & Rectangles page 1 of 2

1 Alexis put two 90° angles together to make a new angle. How many degrees does the new angle measure?

a 90° × 2 = _____

b What kind of angle did Alexis make? Fill in the bubble to show.
- ○ acute angle (less than 90°)
- ○ right angle (exactly 90°)
- ○ obtuse angle (more than 90° but less than 180°)
- ○ straight angle (exactly 180°)

2 Henry put three 45° angles together to make a new angle. How many degrees does the new angle measure?

a 45° × 3 = _____

b What kind of angle did Henry make? Fill in the bubble to show.
- ○ acute angle
- ○ right angle
- ○ obtuse angle
- ○ straight angle

3 Austin put four 15° angles together to make a new angle. How many degrees does the new angle measure?

a 15° × 4 = _____

b What kind of angle did Austin make? Fill in the bubble to show.
- ○ acute angle
- ○ right angle
- ○ obtuse angle
- ○ straight angle

(continued on next page)

Angles & Rectangles page 2 of 2

4 Claudia drew and labeled a rectangle. Here is a miniature picture of her rectangle. Use this picture to help answer the questions below.

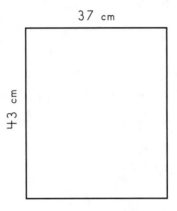

37 cm

43 cm

a What is the sum of the 4 interior angles in Claudia's rectangle? Show your work.

b What is the perimeter of Claudia's rectangle? Show your work.

c What is the area of Claudia's rectangle? Show your work.

d **CHALLENGE** Claudia colored half of her rectangle blue. What is the area of the blue part of the rectangle? Show your work.

Protractor Practice page 1 of 2

When you measure an angle you usually have to choose between two numbers because protractors are designed to measure angles that start on either the right or left side. There are two angles to measure in each of the problems on this sheet and the next. The angle on the left side is angle A. The angle on the right side is angle B. Find and record the measure of both angles in each problem.

1 The measure of angle A is _____ degrees.

The measure of angle B is _____ degrees.

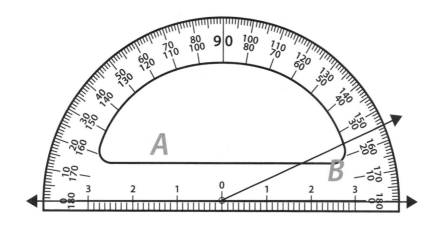

2 The measure of angle A is _____ degrees.

The measure of angle B is _____ degrees.

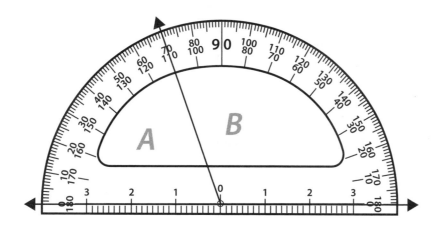

(continued on next page)

93

NAME _____ | DATE _____

Protractor Practice page 2 of 2

3 The measure of angle A is _____ degrees.

The measure of angle B is _____ degrees.

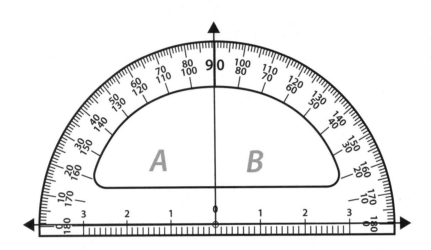

4 The measure of angle A is _____ degrees.

The measure of angle B is _____ degrees.

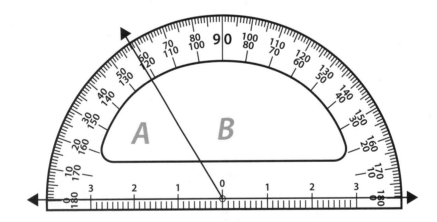

5 Go back and add each pair of angle measures in Problems 1 through 4. What do you notice? Why do you think it works this way?

NAME _____ | DATE _____

 # Drawing Two-Dimensional Figures page 1 of 3

Note to Families

When studying geometry, it is important to understand and be able to use precise language for describing and comparing shapes. In this assignment, students illustrate certain terms and use their understanding of geometry words to draw shapes with different combinations of attributes. We include the vocabulary guide below to refresh your memory and help students remember what the words mean.

Term	Definition	Example
parallel lines	two or more lines that run in either direction and never cross	
perpendicular lines	two or more lines that cross at right angles	
right angle	an angle that measures exactly 90°	
acute angle	an angle that measures between 0° and 90°	
obtuse angle	an angle that measures between 90° and 180°	
quadrilateral	a closed shape with 4 sides	
pentagon	a closed shape with 5 sides	
hexagon	a closed shape with 6 sides	

(continued on next page)

NAME _____ | **DATE** _____

Drawing Two-Dimensional Figures page 2 of 3

1 Draw at least two examples of each term below. If you can't remember what the words mean, look at the guide to geometry terms on page 95.

Term	Your Drawings	
a parallel lines		
b perpendicular lines		
c right angle		
d obtuse angle		
e acute angle		

(continued on next page)

NAME _____ | DATE _____

Drawing Two-Dimensional Figures page 3 of 3

2 Draw at least one shape that matches each description below. For each shape, use arrows and words to show how your shape matches the description.

Description	Your Shape
ex A *quadrilateral* with 2 pairs of *parallel* sides	1st pair of parallel sides · 2nd pair of parallel sides · 4 sides in all makes it a quadrilateral
a A *quadrilateral* with only 1 pair of *parallel* sides	
b A *pentagon* with exactly 1 *right angle* and exactly 1 *acute angle*	
c A *hexagon* with exactly 1 pair of *perpendicular* sides	
d A *hexagon* with exactly 1 pair of *parallel* sides	

NAME | **DATE**

 Symmetry page 1 of 2

1 Figures a–c show only half of the designs, on the left side of their lines of symmetry. Complete each design on the right side of the line of symmetry.

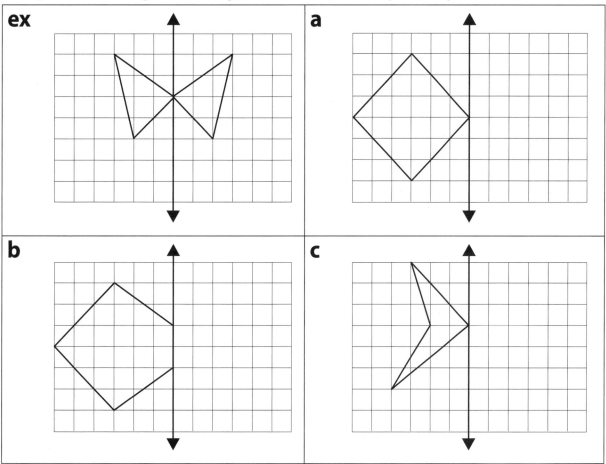

2 What did you do to make sure that the other half of each design you drew was accurate?

Symmetry page 2 of 2

3 Preston says that when a figure has a line of symmetry, the halves on both sides are congruent (exactly the same size and shape). Do you agree or disagree with him? Explain your answer.

4 Tasha says that this shape has 4 lines of symmetry. Do you agree or disagree with her? Explain your answer and be sure to draw in any lines of symmetry you can find. (Hint: Trace the figure, cut it out, and fold it before you make your decision.)

5 **CHALLENGE** Find a picture in the newspaper, in a magazine, or on the computer that has exactly two lines of symmetry. Attach the picture, and then draw in its lines of symmetry. Explain how you would convince someone that it has exactly two lines of symmetry.

NAME _____ |**DATE** _____

 # Classifying & Drawing Quadrilaterals page 1 of 2

A quadrilateral is any polygon that has 4 sides. There are many kinds of quadrilaterals, including these:

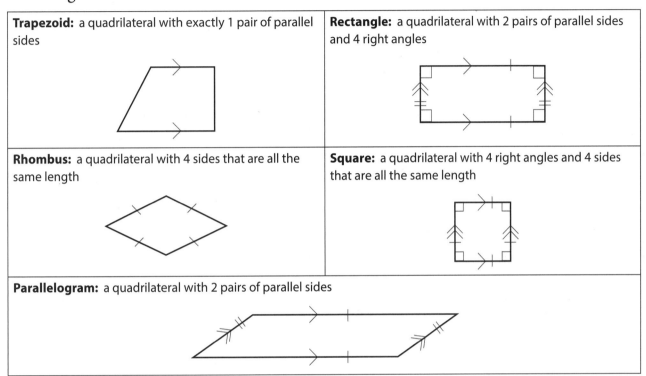

	Trapezoid: a quadrilateral with exactly 1 pair of parallel sides	Rectangle: a quadrilateral with 2 pairs of parallel sides and 4 right angles
	Rhombus: a quadrilateral with 4 sides that are all the same length	Square: a quadrilateral with 4 right angles and 4 sides that are all the same length
	Parallelogram: a quadrilateral with 2 pairs of parallel sides	

1 Look carefully at the figures below. Decide how many right angles, pairs of congruent sides, and pairs of parallel sides each has. Then circle the word or words that say what kind of figure it is. You might circle more than one word for some figures.

Figure	Right Angles?	Pairs of Congruent Sides?	Pairs of Parallel Sides?	Circle the word(s) that describe(s) the figure.
a				trapezoid rectangle rhombus square parallelogram
b				trapezoid rectangle rhombus square parallelogram
c				trapezoid rectangle rhombus square parallelogram

(continued on next page)

 101

NAME | **DATE**

Classifying & Drawing Quadrilaterals page 2 of 2

2 Start with the same line each time to draw the different shapes named below.

ex square

a Parallelogram that is not a rhombus or rectangle

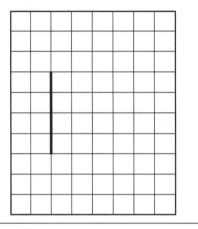

b Trapezoid

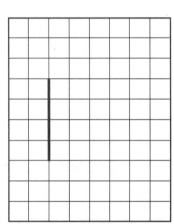

c Rectangle that is not a square

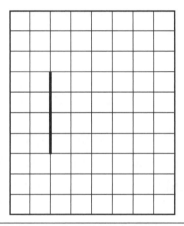

3 **CHALLENGE** Which of your shapes above has the largest area? How can you tell?

NAME _____ | DATE _____

 **Area & Perimeter Review** page 1 of 2

1 Hector says you have to measure the length of every side of this square to find its perimeter. Do you agree with him? Why or why not? Explain your answer.

2 Which equation shows how to find the perimeter of this rectangle?

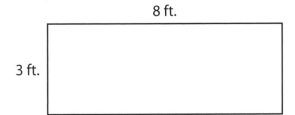

8 ft.

3 ft.

○ $3 \times 8 = 24$ ft.

○ $(2 \times 3) + 8 = 14$ ft.

○ $(2 \times 3) + (2 \times 8) = 22$ ft.

○ $4 + 8 = 12$ ft.

3 Mr. Hunter is trying to find the distance from one end of his whiteboard to the other. Mr. Hunter is measuring:

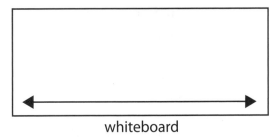

whiteboard

○ the whiteboard's area

○ the whiteboard's length

○ the whiteboard's perimeter

4 Which of these situations is about perimeter?

○ determining the number of tiles needed to cover a floor

○ determining how many feet of fencing is needed to surround a backyard

○ determining the width of a table

5 Beckett and his mom are going to paint the living room. They need to measure the room so they know how much paint to buy. They should measure the wall in:

○ square centimeters

○ square feet

○ square inches

○ square miles

(continued on next page)

NAME _____ | **DATE** _____

Area & Perimeter Review page 2 of 2

6 This rectangle has an area of 45 square feet. What is the missing measure? Show your work.

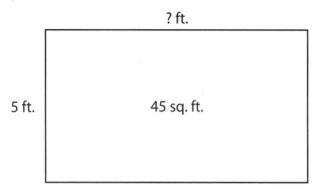

? ft.

5 ft.   45 sq. ft.

7 Tom wants to find the area of his school's basketball court. Which formula should he use? (circle one)

$A = l + w$ $A = l \times w$ $A = l - w$ $A = (2 \times w) + (2 \times l)$

8 Alexandra and her dad built a deck in their backyard. It had an area of 48 square feet and a perimeter of 28 feet. Circle the drawing that shows the deck they built. Use numbers, labeled sketches, and words to explain your answer.

6 ft.

8 ft.

9 ft.

5 ft.

12 ft.

4 ft.

🏠 Area, Perimeter & Multiplication page 1 of 2

1 Jeff is going to hang wallpaper on the big wall in his living room. The wall is 16 feet tall and 23 feet wide. There is a window in the middle of the wall that is 5 feet tall and 8 feet wide. How many square feet of wall does Jeff have to cover with wallpaper? Hint: Draw a picture. Show all of your work.

2 The wallpaper Jeff wants to use comes in rolls that are 1 yard wide and 10 yards long. How many square feet of wallpaper are in each roll? Show all of your work.

3 **CHALLENGE** What happens to the area of a rectangle if you double one side while cutting the other side in half? Start with the rectangle below. Draw and label two more rectangles to show what happens.

```
        8
   ┌──────────┐
 2 │          │
   └──────────┘
```

(continued on next page)

105

NAME _____ | **DATE** _____

Area, Perimeter & Multiplication page 2 of 2

4 Complete each multiplication puzzle. Fill in the products of rows and diagonals.

ex

			35
8	6	1	48
3	5	3	45
7	4	2	56
			80

a

			56
1	6		
4	2		32
4	1		36
			18

b

	3		0
4	2		72
	3	3	45
			42

5 Find the area and perimeter of each figure below.

a

49
38

Area = _____

Perimeter = _____

b

99
75

Area = _____

Perimeter = _____

c

133
46
84   46

Area = _____

Perimeter = _____

6 **CHALLENGE** On a separate piece of paper, draw and label a rectangle with an area of 32 square units and a perimeter of 36 units. Use numbers or words to show that you are correct. Attach the piece of paper to this page.

NAME _____ | DATE _____

 Clock Angles & Shape Sketches page 1 of 2

1 Follow the directions below to construct an angle on each clock face. Use a ruler or a notecard to keep your lines straight. For each one, give the measure of the angle and explain how you know it's that many degrees. (Hint: A circle measures 360°.)

a Draw a line from the point above the 12 to the center of the clock and a line from the center to the point beside the 3.

Angle = _____ °

Here's how I know:

b Draw a line from the point above the 12 to the center of the clock and a line from the center to the point below the 6.

Angle = _____ °

Here's how I know:

c Draw a line from the point above the 12 to the center of the clock and a line from the center to the point beside the 1.

Angle = _____ °

Here's how I know:

d Draw a line from the point above the 12 to the center of the clock and a line from the center to the point beside the 4.

Angle = _____ °

Here's how I know:

(continued on next page)

107   © The Math Learning Center | mathlearningcenter.org

Clock Angles & Shape Sketches page 2 of 2

2 Write instructions to a friend explaining how to sketch a 60° angle on a clock.

3 Danny is learning to make a full turn of 360° on his skateboard. So far, he can make a turn of 270°. How many more degrees does he have to go to make a full turn? Use numbers and a labeled sketch to solve this problem.

4 **CHALLENGE** Sketch the following if they are possible. If they are not possible, explain why they can't be sketched.

a a triangle with parallel sides

b a trapezoid with two lines of symmetry

c a pentagon with two right angles

NAME _____ | **DATE** _____

 Unit 5 Review page 1 of 2

1 Label each item in the box below. Use the words under the box to help you.

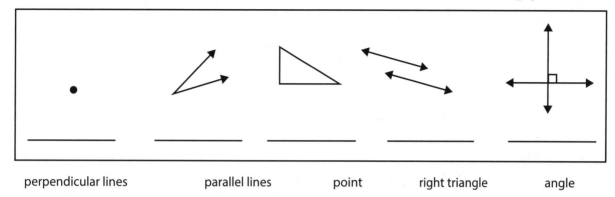

perpendicular lines   parallel lines   point   right triangle   angle

2 Circle the polygons in the box below.

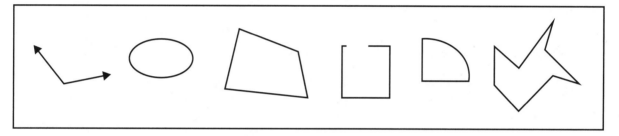

3 Circle the polygons in the box below that have *exactly one* line of symmetry. Then draw in the line of symmetry on each polygon you circled.

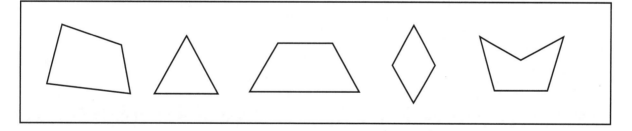

4 A right angle measures 90°. A square has all right angles. Circle the correct word to make each statement true.

a An acute angle measures *more / less* than 90°.

b An obtuse angle measures *more / less* than 90°.

(continued on next page)

Unit 5 Review page 2 of 2

5 Draw an example of the angle described in each box.

an acute angle	a right angle	an angle that measures about 120°

Story Problems

Show your work using numbers, labeled sketches, or words.

6 An ant walked around a rectangular garden. One side of the garden was 16 feet long. The other side was 23 feet long.

a How far did the ant walk? (What was the perimeter of the garden?)

b What was the area of the garden?

7 **CHALLENGE** Clover is mowing her backyard. Her backyard is a rectangle. One side is 60 feet long and the other side is 25 feet long. It took Clover 30 minutes to mow half of her backyard. What is the area of the space that Clover mowed?

NAME _____ | **DATE** _____

 Area & Perimeter Story Problems page 1 of 2

You can make sketches to help solve the problems below. Remember to include the units of measurement in your answers. Show all of your work.

1 The classroom rug is 9 feet long and has an area of 72 square feet. What is the width of the rug?

a What is the perimeter of the rug?

2 Chrissy is going to make a big painting on a piece of wood that is 4 feet wide and has an area of 28 square feet. How long is the piece of wood?

a What is the perimeter of the piece of wood?

3 The school playground measures 465 feet by 285 feet. What is the perimeter of the playground?

(continued on next page)

Area & Perimeter Story Problems page 2 of 2

4 Shanice and Micah are using yellow craft paper to cover a bulletin board. The board is 11 feet wide and 7 feet tall. The craft paper comes in a roll that is 1 yard wide. They can roll it out and cut it to any length, but the paper will always be 1 yard wide. Draw and label on the bulletin board pictures below to show 2 different ways Shanice and Micah can cover the bulletin board.

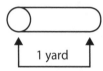

1 yard

a First way.

11 ft.

7 ft.

b Second way.

11 ft.

7 ft.

5 **CHALLENGE** Which of the two ways above wastes less paper? Use pictures, numbers, and words to explain your answer.

NAME _____ | DATE _____

 Fraction Stories page 1 of 2

Fraction Stories

1 Susie wants to make some hot cereal for breakfast. The directions say to use 3 cups of water with 1 cup of cereal to make 4 servings. Susie only wants 1 serving.

a How much cereal should she use? _____

b How much water should she use? _____

c Show your thinking below.

2 The sports store is having a half-off sale where everything is half its original price. Complete the table below. Show your work in the space beside the table.

Original Price	Sale Price
$84	
$56	
$120	
$40.50	
	$42.50
$46.20	
	$71.75

(continued on next page)

113

NAME _____ | **DATE** _____

Fraction Stories page 2 of 2

I weigh 8 pounds, so I need 2 cans a day!

What about me? I weigh 5 pounds, so I need more than 1 can but less than 2. Can you help me out?

3 Missy's mother owns a pet supply store. The directions on the small cans of cat food say to feed a cat 1 can of food each day for every 4 pounds of body weight. Missy started to make a table to help people know how much of this food to give their cats every day. Finish the table.

weight in pounds	cans per day	weight in pounds	cans per day
4	1	10	
5		11	
6		12	
7		13	
8	2	14	
9		15	

114

Conrad's Room page 1 of 2

Think about the most efficient strategy for each problem. Then show your work using numbers, labeled sketches, or words.

1 Conrad is cleaning his room. His bookcase has 7 shelves. He put 18 books on each shelf. How many books did Conrad put away?

2 Conrad's dresser has 6 drawers. He put 13 pieces of clothing in each drawer. How many pieces of clothing did he put away?

3 Conrad has 11 containers for his toys. He put 17 toys in each container. How many toys did he put away?

(continued on next page)

NAME _____ | **DATE** _____

Conrad's Room page 2 of 2

Review

4 Fill in the blanks.

a $\frac{1}{2}$ of 24 is _____   **b** $\frac{1}{4}$ of 24 is _____   **c** $\frac{1}{8}$ of 24 is _____

d $\frac{1}{3}$ of 24 is _____   **e** $\frac{1}{6}$ of 24 is _____   **f** $\frac{1}{12}$ of 24 is _____

5 Fill in the blanks with <, >, or =.

a $\frac{1}{3}$ ▨ $\frac{4}{9}$ **b** $\frac{7}{12}$ ▨ $\frac{4}{8}$

c $\frac{5}{15}$ ▨ $\frac{1}{3}$ **d** $\frac{9}{12}$ ▨ $\frac{2}{3}$

6 **CHALLENGE** Tina collects cans to recycle at the supermarket. Last week, on Monday, Wednesday and Thursday, she collected 37 cans each day. On Tuesday, Friday, Saturday, and Sunday, she collected 43 cans each day. Tina gets 5 cents for every can she recycles.

a How much money did Tina get for her cans last week?

b Tina kept $5 for herself. She divided the rest of the money evenly among her three little brothers. How much money did each brother get?

Paloma's Picture page 1 of 2

Paloma is painting a picture of a house. Help Paloma solve the following problems. Show your work using numbers, sketches, or words.

Hint: Use some of the strategies we have been studying lately to solve these combinations as easily as possible.

1 The door of Paloma's house is 49 millimeters by 24 millimeters. What is the area of the door?

2 One of the windows is 15 millimeters by 32 millimeters. Another window is 30 millimeters by 16 millimeters. Paloma says the windows have the same area. Do you agree or disagree? Why?

3 The porch is 12 centimeters by 19 centimeters. What is the area of the porch?

(continued on next page)

NAME | DATE

Paloma's Picture page 2 of 2

4 Fill in the blanks.

    a $48 \times 25 = 24 \times$ _____

    b $48 \times 29 = (48 \times 30) - (48 \times$ _____ $)$

    c $48 \times 29 = (48 \times 20) + (48 \times$ _____ $)$

    d $50 \times 29 = \frac{1}{2}$ of _____ $\times 29$

5 True or False?

    a $16 \times 17 = 34 \times 8$ _____

    b $39 \times 8 = (40 \times 8) - 1$ _____

    c $64 \times 20 = 32 \times 40$ _____

    d $50 \times 89 = 100 \times 89$ _____

6 **CHALLENGE** Paloma added a garden to her painting. She has 12 rows of flowers. Each row has 13 plants in it. Each plant has 15 flowers on it. How many flowers are in Paloma's garden? Show all your work.

NAME _____ | DATE _____

 Frankie's Fairground page 1 of 2

Frankie goes to the county fair every year. This year, she finds a math problem everywhere she goes. Help Frankie solve the problems. First make an estimate. Then write an equation with a letter standing for the unknown quantity. Finally solve the problem. Show your work using numbers, labeled sketches, or words.

1 Frankie buys 24 tickets to use at the fair. Each ticket costs 25 cents. How much money does Frankie spend on tickets?

Estimate: _____ Equation: _____

Answer: _____

2 Frankie goes on the Ferris wheel first. The Ferris wheel stands on a rectangular platform that has an area of 324 yd² (square yards). One dimension is 9 yards. What is the other dimension?

Estimate: _____ Equation: _____

Answer: _____

(continued on next page)

NAME _____ | DATE _____

Frankie's Fairground page 2 of 2

3 Next, Frankie goes on the Thrill Ride roller coaster. The roller coaster takes up a large rectangular area of the fairground. It is 99 yards on one side and 88 yards on the other side. How much space does the roller coaster take up in square yards?

Estimate: _____ Equation: _____

Answer: _____

4 Write and solve an equation for each of the problems below. Use the table to help.

Measurement Equivalents			
1 kilometer	1,000 meters	10,000 decimeters	100,000 centimeters
	1 meter	10 decimeters	100 centimeters
		1 decimeter	10 centimeters

a How many centimeters are in 45 meters?

b How many meters are in 45 kilometers?

c How many meters are in 800 centimeters?

d CHALLENGE How many decimeters are in 40 kilometers?

Perimeter & Area page 1 of 2

Use labeled sketches and equations to solve the problems on this page and the next.
Show all your work.

1 Josie is putting a fence around her rectangular yard. One dimension measures 24 feet and the other dimension is twice as long. What is the perimeter of Josie's yard?

2 If Josie puts grass in her yard, how many square feet of grass should she buy?

3 Sean measured his rectangular patio and determined the area was 216 square feet. He remembered that one dimension was 9 feet.

a What is the other dimension?

b What is the perimeter of Sean's patio?

(continued on next page)

121

NAME | DATE

Perimeter & Area page 2 of 2

4 Rafael and his sister each drew a rectangle on their driveway. The dimensions of Rafael's rectangle are 16 inches and 24 inches. His sister's rectangle has dimensions of 18 inches and 22 inches.

a Whose rectangle has the larger area?

b By how much?

c Whose rectangle has a larger perimeter?

5 **CHALLENGE** Daria and Luis both drew rectangles. Daria's rectangle has an area of 180 inches and one of the dimensions is 12 inches. Luis's rectangle has a perimeter of 48 inches with one dimension of 13 inches.

a What is the perimeter of Daria's rectangle?

b What is the area of Luis's rectangle?

NAME _____ | **DATE** _____

 Rope Climb Results & Skills Review page 1 of 2

Your P.E. teacher has challenged your class to a rope climb! There are 8 blue pieces of tape equally spaced, and wrapped around the rope to mark off the distances. The following results represent the goal levels that were reached by the students in your group.

$\frac{4}{8}$ $\frac{1}{8}$ $\frac{3}{8}$ $\frac{1}{8}$ $\frac{4}{8}$ $\frac{2}{8}$ $\frac{3}{8}$ $\frac{8}{8}$ $\frac{4}{8}$ $\frac{6}{8}$ $\frac{7}{8}$

1 Display this data on the line plot below. Enter the rest of the goal levels below the heavy line. Make an X above the heavy line to represent each student in your group. Give your finished line plot a good title.

Title _____

Number of Students

$\frac{1}{8}$ $\frac{8}{8}$

Goal Levels Reached Along the Rope

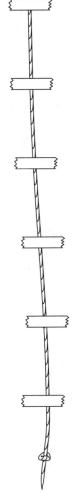

2 How many students stopped at the goal line ⅜?

3 Which goal level did the most students reach?

4 How many students touched or even passed ⅜ of the rope?

5 What was the total distance combined for climbing the rope?

(continued on next page)

123

Rope Climb Results & Skills Review page 2 of 2

6 Solve 216 ÷ 6. Use a ratio table or an array to model and solve the problem.

7 Kevin says that 0.6 is the same as $\frac{6}{10}$. Do you agree or disagree? Why?

8 Write each fraction as a decimal.

$\frac{4}{10} = 0.4$ $\hspace{3cm}$ $\frac{5}{10} =$ $\hspace{3cm}$ $\frac{7}{10} =$

$\frac{25}{100} =$ $\hspace{3cm}$ $\frac{3}{100} =$

10 Write each decimal as a fraction.

$0.31 = \frac{31}{100}$ $\hspace{2.5cm}$ $0.9 =$ $\hspace{2.5cm}$ $0.1 =$

$0.36 =$ $\hspace{2.5cm}$ $0.75 =$

11 Fill in the blanks with <, >, or =.

$\frac{2}{3}$ ▨ $\frac{3}{4}$ $\hspace{2.5cm}$ $\frac{5}{6}$ ▨ $\frac{10}{12}$ $\hspace{2.5cm}$ $\frac{1}{3}$ ▨ $\frac{1}{9}$

$\frac{4}{10}$ ▨ $\frac{1}{2}$ $\hspace{2.5cm}$ $\frac{7}{10}$ ▨ $\frac{75}{100}$

Bakery Bundles page 1 of 2

1 Rachel owns a bakery and sells cookies by the dozen. She sold 16 dozen cookies on Monday. How many cookies did Rachel sell? Show your work.

2 For each dozen cookies, Rachel used $1\frac{1}{2}$ cups of milk. How many cups of milk did she use for 16 dozen cookies? Show your work.

3 A customer ordered 28 cupcakes. What are all the different rectangular arrangements Rachel could use to package the cupcakes? Use labeled sketches to show the possible arrangements below.

4 Rachel's assistant says that $\frac{3}{5}$ cup of oil is more than $\frac{2}{3}$ cup of oil. Is he correct? Explain your reasoning.

(continued on next page)

Bakery Bundles page 2 of 2

5 Rachel uses $\frac{4}{5}$ cup of cocoa for her brownies. Write two fractions that are equivalent to $\frac{4}{5}$.

6 A large order of 240 cookies was placed. How many cookies would go in each box if Rachel put them in the different numbers of boxes listed below? Show your work for each.

a 24 boxes?	**b** 12 boxes?	**c** 6 boxes?

7 **CHALLENGE** Rachel had $\frac{1}{4}$ gallon of milk left in her bakery. She needed to make 4 desserts for an order that afternoon. Use the table to help Rachel decide which dessert she can make 4 of with the milk she has left. Use equations, labeled sketches, or words to prove that your choice will work.

Dessert	Milk needed
Oatmeal Cookies	2 cups
Banana Pie	8 fluid ounces
Apple Cake	12 fluid ounces
Brownies	$2\frac{1}{2}$ cups
Lemon Squares	14 fluid ounces
Shortbread Cookies	16 fluid ounces
Cobbler	$1\frac{1}{2}$ cups

Danny's Data page 1 of 2

Danny collected data about the length of 12 worms he found while he was digging in his yard. Use the data shown on Danny's line plot to answer the questions.

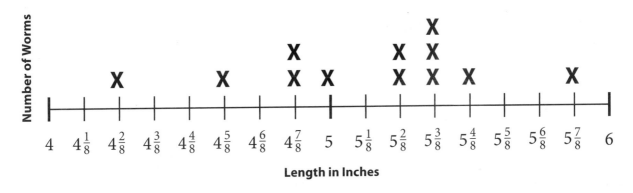

1 What is the range of the data? (The range is difference between the length of the longest and the shortest worm.) Show your work.

2 What is the median (the middle value in the set of X's) of the data?

3 What is the mode (the most common worm length) of the data?

4 What fraction of the 12 worms were less than 5 inches long?

5 What fraction of the worms were longer than $4\frac{7}{8}$ inches but shorter than $5\frac{5}{8}$ inches?

6 What fraction of the worms were more than 5 inches long?

7 If Danny laid the two shortest worms end to end, how long would they be together? Show your work.

8 If Danny put the longest and shortest worm end to end, how long would they be together? Show your work.

(continued on next page)

Danny's Data page 2 of 2

9 Add or subtract these mixed numbers. Show your work.

a $2\frac{1}{3} + 4\frac{2}{3} =$

b $16\frac{5}{8} - 4\frac{3}{8} =$

c $8\frac{4}{7} - 3\frac{5}{7} =$

d $14\frac{5}{9} + 6\frac{7}{9} =$

e $20\frac{1}{8} - 19\frac{7}{8} =$

10 **CHALLENGE**. Danny found one more worm and wanted to add the data to his line plot. He wondered how it would affect the original mode, median and range.

a What is a length the worm could be that would *not* change the mode?

b What is a length that would change the mode?

c What is a length the worm could be that would *not* change the range?

d What is a length that would change the range?

e What is a length the worm could be that would *not* change the median?

f What is a length that would change the median?

Unit 6 Review page 1 of 2

1 If the area of a rectangle is 306 square centimeters (cm²) and one dimension is 6 centimeters, what is the measurement of the other dimension? Use labeled sketches and equations to model and solve this problem.

2 If the area of a rectangle is 612 square centimeters (cm²) and one dimension is 12 centimeters, what is the measurement of the other dimension? Use labeled sketches and equations to model and solve this problem.

3 If the perimeter of a rectangle is 306 centimeters and one dimension is 6 centimeters, what is the measurement of the other dimension? Use labeled sketches and equations to model and solve this problem.

(continued on next page)

129

Unit 6 Review page 2 of 2

4 Six people are splitting the cost of a boat trip. The total is $306. What is each person's share? Show your work.

5 Twelve people are splitting the cost of the same boat trip for a total of $306. Jenny says that each person's share will be half as much as in problem 4. Do you agree with Jenny? Explain your answer, and then solve the problem to prove that you are correct.

6 Three people are splitting the cost of meals on the boat trip. The cost is $153. What is each person's share? Pedro says that the answer to this problem will be the same as the answer to problem 4. Do you agree with Pedro? Explain your answer, and then solve the problem to prove that you are correct.

7 **CHALLENGE** Orlando and his 4 friends joined Michael and his 3 friends in purchasing a gift for their baseball coach. The gift cost $15.75 and the 9 friends split the amount equally. How much did each person spend? Show your work.

NAME _____ | **DATE** _____

 Conversion Tables page 1 of 2

1 Complete the table below and record at least two mathematical observations about the rule and relationship between the measurement conversions.

Meters (m)	Centimeters (cm)
1 m	100 cm
2 m	
	300 cm
4 m	
	500 cm
	600 cm
7 m	

I noticed:

2 A very large bag of frozen vegetables weighs 64 ounces (oz.). How many pounds (lb.) is this? Create a table to show your thinking.

Ounces (oz.)	Pounds (lb.)
16 oz.	1 lb.

Show your thinking another way.

(continued on next page)

Conversion Tables page 2 of 2

3 Solve the conversion problems below. Show your work for each one.

6 ft 7 in = _____ in.	30 ft = _____ yd. _____ ft.
1 yd 2 ft = _____ ft.	32 in = _____ ft. _____ in.
2 ft 4 in = _____ in.	8 ft 6 in = _____ inches

4 Draw a line from each statement on the left to the multiplication equation on the right that matches. Then solve the multiplication equation.

My sister is 4 feet tall. Her height in inches is 12 times as much as 4.

$100 \times 3 =$ _____

My cat weighs 12 pounds. His weight in ounces is 16 times as much as 12.

$12 \times 4 =$ _____

Our rug is 3 meters wide. Its width in centimeters is 100 times as much as 3.

$16 \times 12 =$ _____

5 **CHALLENGE** There are 5,280 feet in a mile. Write your own comparison statement to match this multiplication equation: $5,280 \times 24$. Then solve the equation.

NAME _____ | **DATE** _____

Multiplication Review & Fraction Comparisons page 1 of 2

1 Complete the multiplication problems.

$$\begin{array}{ccccccc} 3 & 3 & 8 & 6 & 3 & 4 & 2 \\ \times\,4 & \times\,3 & \times\,2 & \times\,3 & \times\,8 & \times\,6 & \times\,6 \end{array}$$

2 Represent each fraction on a bar. Then complete each statement with <, >, or = to compare the fractions.

ex

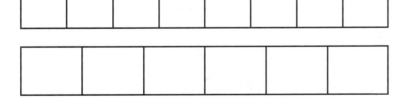

$\dfrac{5}{6} \underline{\quad > \quad} \dfrac{2}{3}$

a

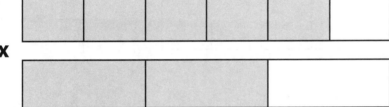

$\dfrac{3}{4} \underline{\qquad} \dfrac{2}{3}$

b

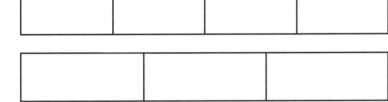

$\dfrac{2}{8} \underline{\qquad} \dfrac{1}{6}$

c

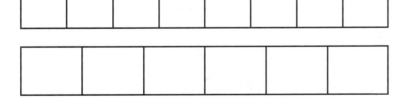

$\dfrac{3}{4} \underline{\qquad} \dfrac{5}{6}$

(continued on next page)

NAME _____ | DATE _____

Multiplication Review & Fraction Comparisons page 2 of 2

3 Use one of the bars below to show a fraction equivalent to $\frac{3}{4}$. Use the other bar to show a fraction equivalent to $\frac{2}{3}$. Think carefully about which bar you'll use for each fraction. Write an equation beside each bar to show the equivalence.

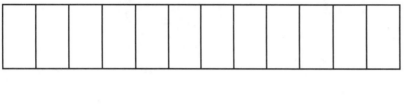

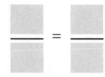

4a **CHALLENGE** Use one of the bars below to show a fraction equivalent to $\frac{4}{5}$. Use the other bar to show a fraction equivalent to $\frac{6}{8}$. Think carefully about which bar you'll use for each fraction. Write an equation beside each bar to show the equivalence.

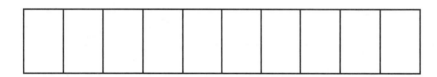

b Draw lines on the bars above to show $\frac{6}{8}$ and $\frac{4}{5}$ with common denominators, and rewrite them here with the common denominator.

$\frac{6}{8}$ = _____ $\frac{4}{5}$ = _____

c Which fraction is larger, $\frac{6}{8}$ or $\frac{4}{5}$? How do you know?

NAME | **DATE**

🏠 Sketch & Compare Fractions

1   Sketch and name two fractions that are equivalent to $\frac{2}{3}$.

$\frac{2}{3}$

a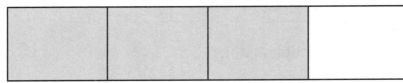

_____

b

_____

2   Sketch and name two fractions that are equivalent to $\frac{3}{4}$.

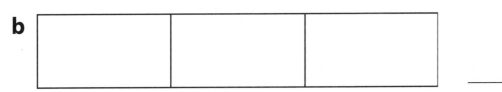

$\frac{3}{4}$

a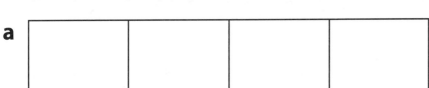

_____

b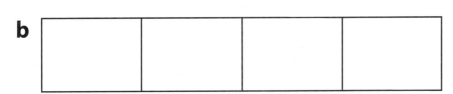

_____

3   Rewrite $\frac{2}{3}$ and $\frac{3}{4}$ with a common denominator.

$\frac{2}{3} =$ _____ $\frac{3}{4} =$ _____

4   Write two statements using <, =, or > to compare $\frac{2}{3}$ and $\frac{3}{4}$.

_____   _____

(continued on next page)

Sketch & Compare Fractions page 2 of 2

5 Sketch and name two fractions that are equivalent to $\frac{1}{4}$.

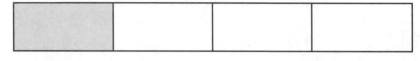

$\frac{1}{4}$

a _____

b _____

6 Sketch and name one fraction that is equivalent to $\frac{3}{10}$.

$\frac{3}{10}$

_____

7 Rewrite $\frac{1}{4}$ and $\frac{3}{10}$ with a common denominator.

$\frac{1}{4} = $ _____ $\frac{3}{10} = $ _____

8 Write two statements using <, =, or > to compare $\frac{1}{4}$ and $\frac{3}{10}$.

_____   _____

9 Rewrite each pair of fractions with a common denominator.
Then write a statement to compare them.

CHALLENGE

ex $\frac{1}{3}$ and $\frac{2}{5}$ **a** $\frac{2}{6}$ and $\frac{3}{8}$ **b** $\frac{5}{6}$ and $\frac{3}{4}$ **c** $\frac{3}{7}$ and $\frac{2}{5}$

$\frac{1}{3} \times \frac{5}{5} = \frac{5}{15}$

$\frac{2}{5} \times \frac{3}{3} = \frac{6}{15}$

$\frac{5}{15} < \frac{6}{15}$, so $\frac{1}{3} < \frac{2}{5}$

NAME | **DATE**

🏠 Fraction Action

1 Label the rest of the tenths and fifths on this number line.

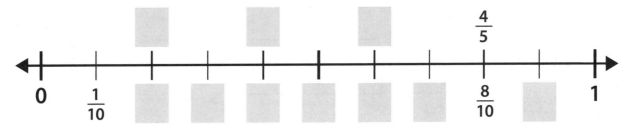

2 Label the fourths on this number line.

3 Use the number lines above to help compare these fractions. Keep in mind that the number lines are exactly the same length. Complete each statement with <, =, or >.

$\frac{5}{10}$ ▢ $\frac{1}{10}$ $\frac{1}{4}$ ▢ $\frac{4}{10}$ $\frac{3}{5}$ ▢ $\frac{2}{4}$ $\frac{4}{5}$ ▢ $\frac{7}{10}$ $\frac{2}{5}$ ▢ $\frac{3}{10}$

4 Represent each fraction on the fraction bar. Then complete the equation to show how much more it would take to make 1.

$\frac{3}{5}$

$\frac{3}{5} + \boxed{} = 1$

$\frac{7}{10}$

$\frac{7}{10} + \boxed{} = 1$

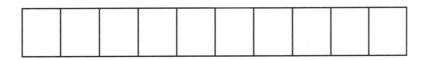

$\frac{5}{8}$

$\frac{5}{8} + \boxed{} = 1$

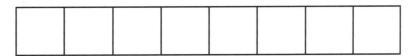

137

NAME _____ | DATE _____

Fraction Action page 2 of 2

5 Represent each fraction on the fraction bar. Then sketch and name an equivalent fraction on the bar below it.

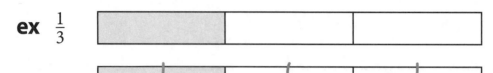

ex $\frac{1}{3}$

$\frac{2}{6} = \frac{1}{3}$

a $\frac{1}{4}$

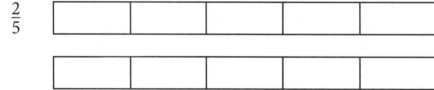

$\boxed{} = \frac{1}{4}$

b $\frac{2}{5}$

$\boxed{} = \frac{2}{5}$

6 Marianna got a long piece of red ribbon from her aunt. She gave $\frac{1}{4}$ of the ribbon to her little sister. She gave $\frac{2}{6}$ of the ribbon to her best friend.

a Who got more of the ribbon, the little sister or the best friend? _____

b Fill in the blank with >, =, or < to complete the comparison. $\frac{1}{4}$ $\frac{2}{6}$

c Use numbers, labeled sketches, or words to show why one of these fractions is greater than the other.

d **CHALLENGE** What fraction of the piece of ribbon did Marianna have left for herself? Show your work.

NAME | **DATE**

 Decimals on Number Lines & Grids page 1 of 2

1 Label each marked point on the number line with a decimal number. Use tenths when you can and hundredths when you must.

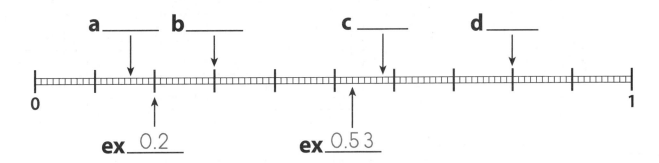

2 Write each number you labeled on the number line beside a grid below. Then shade in the grid to show the decimal amount and write a fraction to represent it.

a

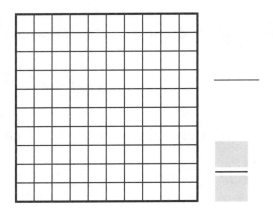

b

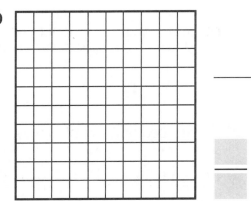

c

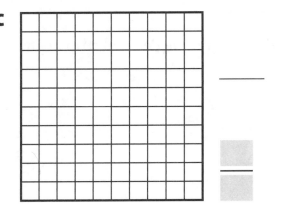

d

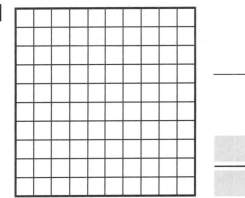

(continued on next page)

NAME _____ | **DATE** _____

Decimals on Number Lines & Grids page 2 of 2

3 Shade each fraction on the grid. Then write an equivalent fraction and two decimal numbers that represent the same amount.

ex $\frac{20}{100}$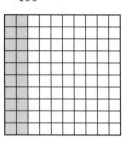

a $\frac{4}{10}$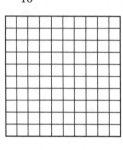

b $\frac{70}{100}$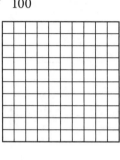

c $\frac{3}{10}$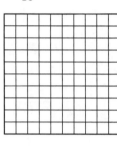

$\frac{2}{10}$ _____ _____ _____

0.2 _____ _____ _____

0.20 _____ _____ _____

4 Write an inequality symbol (< or >) to show which fraction is greater and which is less.

$\frac{20}{100}$ ▮ $\frac{4}{10}$ $\frac{3}{10}$ ▮ $\frac{70}{100}$ $\frac{4}{10}$ ▮ $\frac{70}{100}$ $\frac{20}{100}$ ▮ $\frac{3}{10}$

5 Write an inequality symbol (< or >) to show which decimal is greater and which is less.

0.40 ▮ 0.04   0.89 ▮ 0.9   0.5 ▮ 0.51   0.2 ▮ 0.09

6 Drew says $\frac{3}{10} + \frac{28}{100} = \frac{31}{100}$. Sam says $\frac{3}{10} + \frac{28}{100} = \frac{58}{100}$.

a Who is correct? _____

b How do you know? Include a labeled sketch on the decimal strip below in your explanation.

Standard Algorithms page 1 of 2

1 Use the standard algorithm to solve each multiplication problem.

$\overset{2}{3}4$ × 7 ‾‾‾‾ 238	43 × 6	28 × 4	59 × 4
37 × 3	84 × 3	33 × 8	68 × 5

2 Solve the problems below using the standard algorithm. Show your work.

$\overset{4\,2}{1}64$ × 7 ‾‾‾‾ 1,148	137 × 3	382 × 7	485 × 6
146 × 4	232 × 6	143 × 5	406 × 5

CHALLENGE

1,243 × 5	3,531 × 4	4,325 × 4	3,478 × 9

(continued on next page)

NAME _____ | **DATE** _____

Standard Algorithms page 2 of 2

3 Solve each addition problem using the standard algorithm.

$\overset{1}{}$ 457 + 392 849	403 + 238	573 + 348	226 + 901
2,740 + 342	3,029 + 1,452	4,098 + 3,429	5,768 + 7,431

4 Solve each subtraction problem using the standard algorithm.

$1,\overset{2}{\cancel{3}}\overset{9}{\cancel{0}}5$ − 648 657	638 − 553	503 − 229	1,800 − 925
4,309 − 526	6,005 − 1,347	5,078 − 5,019	2,455 − 1,990

5 **CHALLENGE** Fill in the missing number to make each equation true.

$7,000 = 670 + ($ _____ $\times 5)$ 　　　　 $8,420 = (7 \times$ _____ $) + 797$

$(12 \times 30) - (3 \times$ _____ $) = 114$ 　　　 $($ _____ $\times 25) - 420 = 330$

NAME | DATE

 Choose Your Strategy page 1 of 2

Here are three different ways to solve 4 × 29.

Standard Algorithm	Partial Products	Over Strategy
³ 29 × 4 116	4 × 20 = 80 4 × 9 = 36 80 + 36 = 116	29 is almost like 30. 4 × 30 = 120 120 − 4 = 116

1 Use the standard algorithm to solve each problem below. Then solve it a different way. Label your method. Circle the method that seemed quicker and easier.

		Standard Algorithm	A Different Way
a	39 × 6		
b	51 × 7		
c	65 × 7		
d	199 × 8		

(continued on next page)

Choose Your Strategy page 2 of 2

2 Fill in the bubble to show the best estimate for each problem. Explain your choice.

a   49   ○ 350   **b**   326   ○ 700
      × 8   ○ 400   × 3   ○ 800
               ○ 450   ○ 900
               ○ 500   ○ 1,000

c Circle the method that seems to help most for estimating the answers to these problems.

Standard Algorithm   Partial Products   Over Strategy   Rounding

3 Sam, Sarah, Deena, and TJ each have 37 marbles. How many marbles do they have in all? Write and solve an equation for this problem. Show all your work.

4 **CHALLENGE** The kids at the high school are having a monthlong car wash. They charge $6.00 to wash a car. If they wash 28 cars a day for 9 days, how much money will they make? Write and solve an equation for this problem. Show all your work.

NAME _____ | DATE _____

 Variables & Expressions page 1 of 2

Sometimes people use letters to represent unspecified amounts. Such letters are called variables. For example, if you worked for $6 an hour, you would multiply the time you worked by 6 to find out what you earned. If we let t represent the time you worked, we could show the amount of money you earned with this expression.

$$6 \times t$$

When we say, "evaluate the expression when $t = 3$," we mean, "figure out how much money you would make if you worked for 3 hours." To do this, substitute 3 for t and complete the calculation.

1 Evaluate the expression $6 \times t$ when:

$t = 2$ $t = 4$

$t = 5$ $t = 8$

2 How much money would you make if you worked 15 hours and earned $6 per hour?

3 Evaluate the following expressions when each variable has the value shown.

$4 + b$ when $b = 10$ $4 + 10 = 14$	
$4 + b$ when $b = 23$	$4 + b$ when $b = 103$
$(3 \times n) - 2$ when $n = 2$	$(3 \times n) - 2$ when $n = 4$
$2 \times (k + 12)$ when $k = 7$	$2 \times (k + 12)$ when $k = 10$

(continued on next page)

145

Variables & Expressions page 2 of 2

4 Danny is trying to earn money to buy a new bike. His neighbor says he will pay him $4 per hour to help with yard work. His mom says she will give him a $10 bill to add to his savings after he helps his neighbor. Which expression shows how much money Danny will make? (The letter h stands for the number of hours Danny will work for his neighbor.)

$4 + h + 10$ $4 \times h + 10 \times h$ $4 \times h + 10$ $14 \times h$

a How much money will Danny make if he works for 4 hours with his neighbor? Show all your work.

b If Danny wants to earn $34, how many hours will he have to work? Show all your work.

5 **CHALLENGE** Pick one of the expressions from problem 3 above that does not represent Danny's situation. Describe a situation where the expression you chose would represent how much money Danny would make.

a The expression I chose is:

b This expression would show how much money Danny would make if…

Unit 7 Review page 1 of 2

Here are some problems about the function machine.

1a Set the function machine's controls to multiply each input number by 4 and then subtract 2. One has been done for you. (You get to choose and write in the last 4 input numbers yourself.)

in	out
3	10
4	
10	
2	
6	
24	

b Choose the equation that best represents this rule.

○ ($\boxed{\text{in}}$ − 2) × 4 = $\triangle_{\text{out}}$

○ ($\boxed{\text{in}}$ × 4) − 2 = $\triangle_{\text{out}}$

○ ($\boxed{\text{in}}$ × 2) − 4 = $\triangle_{\text{out}}$

2a Now set the machine's controls to make each output number 5 times as much as the input number. One has been done for you. Choose and write in the last input number yourself.

in	out
10	50
15	
20	
25	
30	
35	
40	
45	
50	

b Describe 2 different patterns you notice in the output numbers.

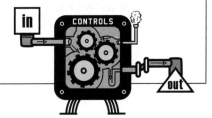

3 Solve these multiplication problems.

$$\begin{array}{r} 40 \\ \times\ 80 \\ \hline \end{array} \qquad \begin{array}{r} 400 \\ \times\ \ 8 \\ \hline \end{array} \qquad \begin{array}{r} 30 \\ \times\ 50 \\ \hline \end{array} \qquad \begin{array}{r} 90 \\ \times\ 70 \\ \hline \end{array} \qquad \begin{array}{r} 60 \\ \times\ 60 \\ \hline \end{array}$$

(continued on next page)

147

Unit 7 Review page 2 of 2

4 Marco says he can solve 83 × 49 by multiplying 80 × 49 and 3 × 49 and then adding them together.

a Do you agree or disagree? Explain.

b Would you solve 83 × 49 with Marco's strategy or a different strategy? Explain. Then solve the problem and show all your work.

5 Kaya is sorting the beads in her bead collection. She has a box with 32 different sections. She puts 19 beads in each section. How many beads did Kaya put in her box?

a Write an equation with a letter to show the number of beads Kaya put in her box.

b Solve the problem. Show your work using numbers, sketches, or words.

6 **CHALLENGE** Kaya has another box with 46 sections. She puts 18 beads in half of the sections and 21 beads in the other half. How many beads did Kaya put in this box? Show your work.

🏠 Another Grassy Field page 1 of 2

1 The 32 students in Ms. Li's class are planting grass for their science project.

a What are all the different ways the students can arrange their 32 milk carton containers of grass in a rectangular field? Circle the dimensions that you think would look most like a field for a playground.

b Each container's base has a length and width of $3\frac{3}{4}$ inches. What is the length and width of the entire field? Sketch the rectangular field and record the dimensions. Show all your work.

c What is the area of the field formed by the cartons of grass? Show all your work.

(continued on next page)

149

Another Grassy Field page 2 of 2

2 Four new students joined Ms. Li's class.

a What are all the possible dimensions of the field now?

b Write the dimensions you would choose for a field. Then, find the length and width of that field in inches.

3 **CHALLENGE** What is the area of Ms. Li's class' field after the four new students' cartons of grass have been added?

| DATE

 Ten-Foot Seesaw page 1 of 2

Mr. Sanchez's class conducted an experiment with a model seesaw using a pencil, ruler, and tiles. (The tiles represent pounds of weight, so if the seesaw lifts 60 tiles, the real seesaw would lift 60 pounds.) Their results are in the table below.

Weight on One End (tiles or pounds)	Fulcrum Position	Weight Needed to Lift (tiles or pounds)
60	4 inches	30
60	5 inches	40
60	6 inches	60
60	7 inches	80
60	8 inches	120

1 The class has a real seesaw on their playground that is 10 feet long. Their model seesaw is 12 inches long.

a What is the length of their real seesaw in inches? Show your work using words, numbers, or labeled sketches.

b What is the difference in length between the real and model seesaws?

2 Fill in the diagram to help Mr. Sanchez's class figure out where to place the fulcrum on their real 10-foot seesaw.

Scale Diagram

0 in.   4 in.   5 in.   6 in.   7 in.   8 in.   12 in.

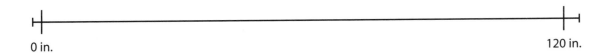

0 in.   120 in.

Ten-Foot Seesaw page 2 of 2

3 Where should the class place the fulcrum on the real seesaw for a 120-pound 10th grader to balance with a 60-pound 4th grader?

    a How many feet is that from the end of the seesaw? Draw a picture to show your thinking.

4 Where should the class place the fulcrum on the real seesaw for a 60-pound 4th grader to balance with a 40-pound 1st grader?

    a How many feet is that from the end of the seesaw? Draw a picture to show your thinking.

Circle Explorations page 1 of 2

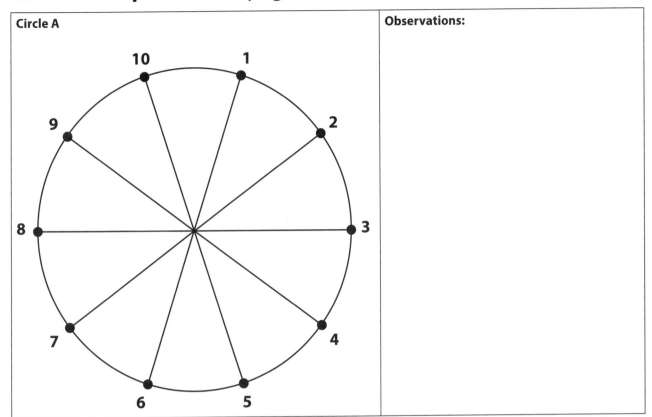

Circle A

Observations:

Directions for Circle A

1 Use a ruler to draw line segments to connect each numbered point on the circumference of circle A. Draw a line from point 1 to point 2, from point 2 to point 3, and so on.

2 The polygon you have just drawn is called a decagon because it has 10 sides.

3 Each numbered point on this circle has a partner right across the circle from it. Draw line segments to connect each point to the points on either side of its partner.

For example: Point 1's partner across the circle is point 6. You will draw a line segment connecting point 1 to point 5. Then draw another line segment connecting point 1 to point 7.

4 Do this for all 10 points on the circumference of circle A.

5 Write at least three mathematical observations about the figure you've just drawn.

153

NAME _____ | DATE _____

Circle Explorations page 2 of 2

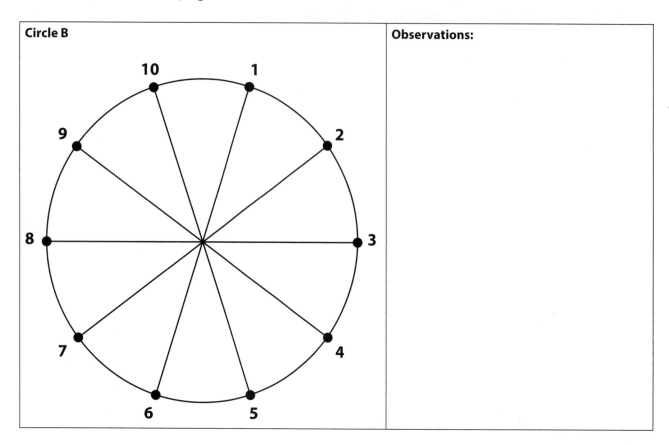

Circle B

Observations:

Directions for Circle B

1 Now use a ruler to draw line segments to connect only the even-numbered points on the circumference of circle B. Do not connect the odd-numbered points. Draw a line from point 2 to point 4, from point 4 to point 6, from point 6 to point 8, and so on.

2 How many sides are in the polygon you have just drawn inside circle B? _____
What is the name of a polygon with this many sides? _____

3 Each numbered point on circle B has a partner right across the circle from it.

4 Draw line segments to connect each even-numbered point to the points on either side of its partner.

For example Point 2's partner is point 7. You will draw a line segment connecting point 2 to point 8. Then draw another line segment connecting point 2 to point 6.

5 Do this for all five even-numbered points on the circumference of circle B.

6 Write at least three mathematical observations about the figure you've just drawn.

7 **CHALLENGE** Design a color scheme and color both figures with colored pencils or felt pens.

Most Important Items page 1 of 2

Ms. Li's class added their teams' tallies of their most important playground items to this chart.

Playground Item	Tallies	Total
swings	5 + 3 + 1 + 2 + 1	
play structure	18 + 12 + 7 + 5 + 10	
slide	4 + 5 + 3 + 2 + 6	
tetherball	2 + 3	
climbing wall	18 + 26 + 10 + 16 + 2	
sliding bars	8 + 3 + 18 + 4 + 3	
seesaw	9 + 8 + 4	
hanging bars	7 + 6 + 1 + 2	
basketball hoop	11 + 22 + 15 + 5 + 9	

1 Find the total points for each playground item, and add the totals to the table above. Show two different strategies for adding the numbers efficiently. Work on a second piece of paper if you need more space.

2 Chart the total data you calculated above on a bar graph. Remember to choose a scale and label it and to give your graph a title.

(continued on next page)

Most Important Items page 2 of 2

3 Which item does Ms. Li's class think is most important? Explain your thinking.

4 Which item does Ms. Li's class think is least important?

5 What is the range of the data?

Pricing Playground Equipment page 1 of 2

The Waterton School District asked two building companies to estimate pricing for the items they want to include on a new playground.

1 Find the average cost of each item and enter the costs on the table below. Use the space below the table to show your work.

Items	Bob's Building Price	Pat's Playgrounds Price	Average Cost
Climbing Wall	$3,830	$5,642	
Tetherball	$567	$645	
Play Structure	$7,635	$6,789	
Foursquare Courts	$456	$578	
Twisty Slide	$2,750	$2,369	
Swings	$2,599	$3,050	

(continued on next page)

Pricing Playground Equipment page 2 of 2

2 What is the total of the average costs of the playground project?

3 The school district needs to set a budget for the project. What should the budget be? Use numbers and words to justify your answer.

4 The school district would prefer to have just one builder do the whole project. If they have to use one of these two builders, which builder should they choose? Use numbers and words to justify your answer.

🏠 Measurement & Decimal Review page 1 of 2

1 Read the situations below carefully. Write E if an estimate is good enough. Write M if a precise measurement is necessary.

a _____ Isaac is buying some items at the store. He has $20 in his pocket. Does he need to know exactly how much the items cost altogether, or can he estimate to see if he has enough money?

b _____ Tiffany is making a frame for her favorite picture. Does she need to measure the picture exactly to know how big her frame should be, or can she estimate?

c _____ Martin has some chores he needs to do on Saturday. His friend wants to know if he can come over to play at 4:30. Does Martin need to know exactly how long he will spend on each chore, or can he estimate to see if he will be done in time to play with his friend?

d _____ Jin is baking cookies. Can he estimate the amount of flour he puts in the recipe, or does he need to measure it out exactly?

e _____ Mrs. Suarez is making some curtains for her living room. Can she estimate how big her windows are, or should she measure them to figure out exactly how wide and tall they are before she starts cutting her fabric?

2 Describe a time you needed to take an exact measurement. What were you doing? What tool did you use to measure? What unit of measurement did you use?

3 Describe a time you made an estimate. How did you make your estimate? For example, did you use rounding and friendly numbers? Did you think about what you already knew?

(continued on next page)

NAME _____ | DATE _____

Measurement & Decimal Review page 2 of 2

4 Write the decimal number that is equal to each fraction below.

$\frac{1}{2}$ =	$1\frac{1}{2}$ =	$\frac{6}{10}$ =	$\frac{79}{100}$ =
$\frac{1}{4}$ =	$\frac{3}{4}$ =	$\frac{7}{10}$ =	$\frac{2}{100}$ =
$\frac{30}{100}$ =	$\frac{53}{100}$ =	$2\frac{6}{100}$ =	$2\frac{1}{4}$ =

5 Use >, <, or = to compare each pair of numbers.

$\frac{3}{2}$ ▢ 1.5	0.6 ▢ $\frac{9}{100}$	$\frac{36}{100}$ ▢ 0.25	0.75 ▢ $\frac{9}{12}$
$83\frac{1}{2}$ ▢ 83.48	$\frac{125}{100}$ ▢ 1.07	$\frac{82}{100}$ ▢ 0.9	$74\frac{3}{4}$ ▢ 74.8

6 Shade in and label each grid to show a decimal number that fits the description. There is more than one right answer for each one.

Show a number that is greater than $\frac{1}{2}$ and has an odd number in the hundredths place.	Show a number that is greater than $\frac{3}{4}$ and has a 0 in the hundredths place.
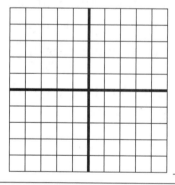	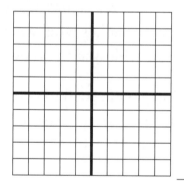
Show a number that is less than $\frac{1}{4}$ and has an even number in the tenths place.	Show a number between $\frac{1}{4}$ and $\frac{1}{2}$ with an odd number in the tenths place.
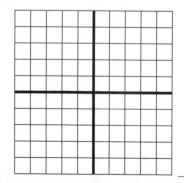	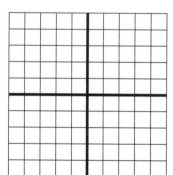

160

NAME **_____** | DATE **_____**

 Drawing the Playground page 1 of 2

Ms. Li's class drew a scaled map of the area they needed for their play structure. The rectangle below represents the playground with measurements to 1:360 scale.

1 What is the length, width, perimeter, and area of the space at full scale? Give the dimensions in centimeters and meters.

	Centimeters	Meters
Length		
Width		
Perimeter		
Area		

8 cm

5 cm

(continued on next page)

Drawing the Playground page 2 of 2

2 The merry-go-round drawing below is to 1:24 scale. What is the diameter of the merry-go-round at full scale? Give the diameter in centimeters and meters.

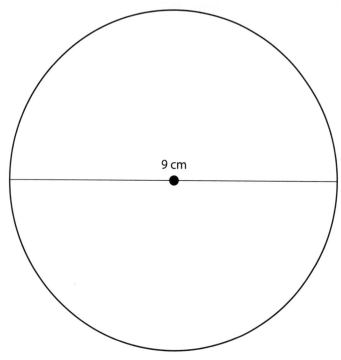

9 cm

3 The drawing of a seesaw platform below is to 1:50 scale. What is the length, width, perimeter, and area of the seesaw at full scale? Give the dimensions in centimeters and meters.

6 cm

1 cm

	Centimeters	Meters
Length		
Width		
Perimeter		
Area		

162

Playground Map page 1 of 2

Ms. Vega's class has a playground with a length of 50 meters and a width of 40 meters.

1 Draw a large outline for a map of the playground below.

(continued on next page)

NAME _____ | DATE _____

Playground Map page 2 of 2

2 Arrange all of the following items on the playground map. Make sure their dimensions fit in the playground space. You do not have to draw the map precisely to scale.

- Label each item on your map.

- Find the area of each item and enter it in the table below.

Playground Item	Dimensions	Area of Each Item
Play Structure	20 meters × 25 meters	
Slide	7 meters × 20 meters	
Swings	18 meters × 11 meters	
Climbing Wall	21 meters × 8 meters	
Seesaw	5 meters × 7 meters	
Basketball Court	20 meters × 15 meters	
Merry-Go-Round	4 meters × 4 meters	

3 Add your choice of additional playground items to the remaining space on your map. Write the name, dimensions, and area of each additional item in the table.

NAME | **DATE**

Designing Playground Equipment

1 Design and draw a picture of an original piece of playground equipment. Include and label at least three simple machines.

Notes

Notes

Notes

Notes

Notes

Notes